Going Home and Other Tales from Guyana

Short Stories by
Deryck M Bernard

MACMILLAN
CARIBBEAN

Going Home and Other Tales from Guyana is a highly entertaining book of short stories in the Macmillan Caribbean Writers Series, an exciting new collection of fine Caribbean writing with special appeal for readers in their teens and twenties. These tales recall boyhood days in colonial British Guiana, the amorous exploits of young men, adventures digging for gold in the bush, cricket at Bourda and a host of eccentric characters.

Macmillan Caribbean Writers fiction reads easily, tells a good story and each title focuses on some aspect of the Caribbean youth experience, exploring the hardships, challenges and achievements of growing up in a small community of many immigrant peoples.

As well as short stories, the Series includes novellas, poetry anthologies and collections of plays particularly suitable for Arts and Drama Festivals. There are also works of non-fiction such as an eye-witness account of life under the volatile Soufriere volcano.

The Series introduces the work of a new generation of writers, and in addition introduces new work by established authors. The first dozen writers aboard the Macmillan Caribbean Writers list come from all around the region, including Guyana, Trinidad, Tobago, Bequia, St. Lucia, Dominica, Montserrat, Antigua, the Bahamas, Jamaica and Belize.

These titles are carefully selected to meet the present need for well-written, gripping stories, with familiar themes and settings, that today's Caribbean youth can genuinely enjoy reading. The maturer general reader of West Indian literature too will find much of interest in this innovative series from Macmillan Caribbean.

The Macmillan Caribbean Writers Series
Caribbean writing for young adults
edited by Judy Stone

Novellas:
Martina Altmann: Jeremiah, Devil of the Woods
Joanne C Hillhouse: The Boy from Willow Bend

Plays:
Judy Stone (ed): Champions of the Gayelle
Alwin Bully: Good morning, Miss Millie
Zeno Constance: Duelling Voices
Pat Cumper: The Rapist

Stories:
Deryck M Bernard: Going Home and Other Tales from Guyana
Jan Carew: The Sisters, and Manco's Stories

Macmillan Education
Between Towns Road, Oxford OX4 3PP
A division of Macmillan Publishers Limited
Companies and representatives throughout the world

www.macmillan-caribbean.com

ISBN 0 333 95304 5

Typeset by EXPO Holdings
Cover design by AC Design
Cover illustration by Philbert Gajadhar

Printed in Malaysia

2006   2005   2004   2003   2002
10   9   8   7   6   5   4   3   2   1

CONTENTS

1	Ben	1
2	Black Water	6
3	Big Joe	11
4	Bourda	15
5	Choker	21
6	Going Home	27
7	Photographs	32
8	Sonny Coming	36
9	Sugrim, Patrick and Me	39
10	The Big Fight	43
11	The Dance	48
12	The Visitation	53
	Guyanese Glossary	57

Ben

M y aunt Hildred spent a lot of time disapproving. She disapproved of dances and parties. She disapproved of cricket on Sundays and football at any time. She disapproved of calypso music. She disapproved of loud laughter. She was always alert to cut short any sign of happiness or joy in me. Signs of beauty and flirtatiousness in my sister, Irene, were a particular worry to the old lady. Aunt Hildred approved of church. An Anglican, she went to all masses, services, bible classes, mother's union and any other activities the priest could devise for parishioners like Auntie. Easter Holy Week was enjoyment unconfined for aunt Hildred. Here was church every afternoon for a whole week, where they sang depressing hymns about crimson tides and deepest, bitterest agony, taking Auntie to heights of pleasure.

I never did quite understand why my mother sent me to live for so many years with Hildred, for my mother did not resemble her in any way. My mother was a fun-loving woman who laughed a lot and was always keen on a good time. She led an active party life well into a disreputable middle age. She never married my father and enjoyed the company of many "uncles", some of whom I have heard wished to marry her and make her a respectable matron. Yet she believed that life with the dreaded Hildred was necessary to make me a better person and teach me the respectability which she despised.

Hildred owned a cake shop, which sold a wide assortment of bottled drinks, cakes and buns, sweets and a limited range of groceries. She presided over this domain, fierce and large-breasted, with a permanent frown and a deep voice. She maintained her reign of terror every day except Sundays, when she was off to church or other holy entertainment. Hildred believed in manners. She demanded a loud and clear "Good afternoon" or "Good morning" before she considered your application for bread. And you had to give a loud "Thank you, Miss Hildred" after you had paid and received your change. If you did not come up to her expectations of good manners, she was liable to drive you from her manor forthwith, with severe injunctions concerning your future conduct. The protocol surrounding Hildred's shop was intense.

"Good afternoon, Miss Hildred. Mummy sent to say good afternoon and if you could please send her three eight-cents loaves of bread, please and thanks."

I often wondered whether Hildred realised that her customers intended to pay. If you wanted to shop at "Laughie", the Chinese grocer at the other end of the street, you need not wish him "Good afternoon" at all. He was not interested in manners or behaviour, and would laugh at the dirty jokes of the less respectable customers, and gave you discounts and trust in hard times. Nor did he care if you brought a bag in which to put your purchases. Hildred would refuse to sell to you if you turned up for your buns or drinks without a bag. She boasted that she had never in her life served anyone without a bag. She also sold mauby and pine in small glasses, and would not allow you to use your finger to stir the ice. It was a mystery to me that anyone would want to enter her shop at all unless compelled by parental orders.

Ben turned up just before Easter. Ben was a tall, grizzled and hirsute Barbadian of imprecise middle age, with a gravelly voice and the most contemptible manners. He spat, swore and drank. He told the most disgusting stories about women who hung around the waterfront and bush camps. He arrived one morning in the shop, was greeted with joy by aunt Hildred and was installed in the little spare room at the back. I could not believe that my aunt would even know a man like that let alone be willing to keep him. But she was obviously glad to see him and fed him luxuries like tinned salmon and saltfish choka and foo-foo and split peas soup with cowheel. Hildred was very nice to Ben. She even smiled at him, a charming – even wicked – smile that I had never seen before.

I admired Ben. He took me under his wing and taught me many things a young boy needed for a happy childhood. Ben knew how to make tops, paper kites, model boats. He could make and throw cast-nets for the patwa and houri fish from the canals which abounded in our village. Ben was an expert in tying knots and catching yawaries from the crowns of the coconut trees. He could cook peas and rice on a small bush fire in the back yard. He knew which fruits growing in the bush beyond the back-dam were good to eat. He knew how to use its palms to make baskets and which trees in the back-dam made good walking sticks. To Ben, the killing of snakes was child's play, and feeling for crabs in the mudflats over our sea wall was no problem. Ben also played the harmonica, which we called the mouth organ, and knew beautiful tunes which he called "blues". My school friends and I could listen to him all night as he played the haunting lines, sitting with his legs dangling over the side of the bridge to the shop. And Ben never had to go to church. He was contemptuous of all religion, and of the vicar in particular. He drank and swore on Sundays and delighted in telling his most obscene stories when Hildred had respectable church people in the shop. He displayed no sign of formal manners or gentility but did have a certain charm, for I noticed that even the most grim-faced of the mother's union, even fat Miss Ethel, a sad and holy sister from the "Assemblies" on the West Road, would yield to his humour and insinuations. He was extremely crude. He was allowed to make jokes about their teeth, behinds and bosoms, as well as some other parts with names that I did not recognise. I assumed that respectability would break out, and Ben would be brought to heel, but it never did.

Who was Ben? Why was he allowed to behave this way without censure from my aunt and her henchwomen? How did my aunt come to know a man like that? Why did she feed him and accommodate him? Why was he allowed to make jokes about her behind using words which had earned me a licking on numerous occasions? And what was there about Ben which allowed the suspension of all the usual moral certainties?

Old Miss Harris, the ancient Bajan lady who gave music lessons on the public road, died suddenly. Miss Harris was a prominent member of the Methodist church and a stalwart of all respectable village institutions, including the burial society and the Party. Her death was a great occasion, with the well-attended wake and funeral a chance for Hildred to spend a lot of time with her holy friends. She dragged me off to the wake at the Harris house. The men hung round under the house drinking rum and high-wine. They played dominoes, noisily slapping them on the make-shift tables. The women went upstairs and sang hymns. The singing of our women at wakes is a scary business. All the years of poverty, deprivation and abuse were expressed as the mournful sounds of "Peace, perfect peace", "Abide with me" and other suitable dirges were wailed. The more prominent singers had a knack of dragging the long vowels, and it gives me goose-pimples even to recall those long nights. Some singers made a pretence of singing in harmony, which was even more painful than the nasal dragging of the melody. Mr Grimes, who alternated between the domino games and rum downstairs and the singing upstairs, added many absurd noises which my aunt advised me were known as "singing solfa". It was proof of his great learning and cultural exposure.

A wake has certain formalities which must be obeyed. New arrivals needed to proclaim how they heard of Miss Harris's demise, and Miss Harris's nieces would describe the last hours of the old lady's life and her last words, which became more pious and embellished as the night progressed. Then at nine o'clock, everyone went quiet as the radio was turned up to play the list of death announcements and messages. They all knew that Miss Harris was dead but listened solemnly anyway, and we youngsters were kept in severe silence. Miss H was second on the list and it was noted with satisfaction that she had many friends and relations in a long and impressive announcement. But there was a strange bit of information. Miss Harris had one son – Benjamin Aloisus Harris – and it took me several seconds to make the connection.

Ben slouched into the wake house shortly afterwards. To my surprise he joined the hymn singing, and my whole assessment of him was completely and irrevocably overturned. Ben had the sweetest voice I had ever heard in my life. I now know that what he had was a rich bass-baritone. He sang in tune. He sang beautifully, with a care for the words and enunciation that made all our respectable church choristers sound pathetic, rustic and crude. It carried all over the village. People heard him who lived by the train. He knew the words of all the hymns and he sang leaning casually on the wall near the kitchen, silencing all the talking, quietening the slap of dominoes and hushing the hum of rum drinking downstairs. I have paid good money in London and Paris to hear men sing in concert halls, and few of them moved me with the power of Ben that night. Then just as he started, he stopped and went downstairs to join the high-wine drunkards under the house. He passed out just after midnight and slept the sleep of the drunk for the rest of the wake.

Ben left early next morning and carried his few belongings with him. By the time of the funeral later that afternoon, auntie Hildred was back to her respectable self and was prominent at the graveside, comforting the relations, giving smelling-salts to the fainting, and restraining the excesses of Elvira's nieces, who kept attempting to throw themselves into the excavation. When Miss H's lawless niece-in-law from Berbice threw herself to the ground in her grief, and her petticoat and garters were exposed to public view, she dealt with the matter firmly, lest worse moral disaster befall and more intimate apparel be exposed. Ben and other distractions had passed as a fleeting mirage.

I could not bear the mystery for very long and on my next visit to my mother I very shyly raised the question of Ben, Hildred and Miss Harris. She laughed her raucous laugh, which Hildred called her disgusting "belly laugh", and informed me that I was getting big and should know the "facts". She proceeded to tell me an incredible story. Miss Harris was a respectable young teacher with a great future and a college certificate, born to a family of Barbadian Methodists. Tragically, however, she had fallen and "Ben", that gruff scapegrace, was the result. Her career path to headteachership of a church school was closed, but Ben was groomed for a respectable life. He did brilliantly in the church school, was a gifted musician, and grew to be an excellent speaker. A career as a teacher, parson or even lawyer was considered well within his grasp. Vast sums were saved and invested in his passage to London, where the paths to greatness lay. Ben, however, was not interested in a career or in education or respectability, and certainly had no intention of becoming a parson. Instead, he re-enacted the tale of the prodigal and brought shame and disgrace on all concerned, returning to the colony penniless and unqualified. He was, however, interested in Hildred, who was at that time one of the great beauties of the village. At this point in the story my mother was not very clear, but I gather that the scandalous liaison – replete with shocking sightings on the sea wall in darkest night – only ended when Ben abandoned Hildred to take up life as an itinerant labourer in the bush, and Hildred became a premature old woman in a cake shop. I try to imagine aunt Hildred recklessly in love with a young Ben, and a disgraced and scandal-ridden Miss Harris. I have never managed it.

I never saw Ben again. There is a rumour that he died penniless up river, but others claim that he went to Barbados, his mother's place of origin, and lived to a ripe and happy old age.

Black Water

I have always claimed that she was the most beautiful woman I ever met. Lennox, who never saw her, is sceptical and puts it down to the effects of youth, inexperience, seasickness, and tiredness from a rough journey. Believe me, it was a rough journey to the river. I have not been back to BG for many years and things may have changed, though I doubt it. There were two ways to get to the landing by the river of black water. You could go by the government ferry, but to do that you needed two days and a stomach cast in iron, and the capacity to fall asleep standing up, or in a wildly swinging hammock if you found room. The ferry headed out to sea and for one day you got accustomed to a right-to-left roll, and when your body had settled and your stomach had ceased heaving, the ferry turned in the other direction and headed to the river and tossed left-to-right instead.

Fred and I did the trip in our early days in the service. He saw Hermina and deep in his heart he knew that she was an angel, but I think that he was peeved because she took no notice of him, he being the usual "sweetboy" in our band. Whenever this story comes up, he remains vague, unable to stifle his conscience but unwilling to make an admission that would make me look good.

You could go to the landing by a fast, high ballahoo. These were fitted with two big outboard engines and two drums of gasoline. The torture was more intense, for the Atlantic kicked the ballahoo much worse than it did the ferry, but then the suffering was half as long. The boat bounced randomly on the waves as you lost sight of the mangroves and the palms. The sea became a lighter brown, the fish became bold and jumped above the surface. When you approached the coast again, heading for the river of black water, you saw the dark green of the palm forest and big sea birds pass over your head and you said a silent Our Father. You knew you would not drown this time. If you tried the journey in the ballahoo by night or in the rainy season, you had to pray all the time anyway.

After the torture by high seas and cold winds and dousing in seawater, the last bit of the trip on the river was like a pleasure cruise. The mangrove reached into the water and you rarely saw land except where there was an estate growing coconuts or limes or coffee, and the huts where the Warrau people had their fishing villages. The further up the river you went, the darker the water became until it was dark red, almost black, the sweet water of the bush. The landing was 30 miles up the river and the government house overlooked the water just fifty yards from the landing. In this part of the world, young though we were, we had VIP treatment and the privileges reserved for senior public servants.

The rest-house was built at the beginning of the century by an ambitious colonial magistrate who hoped that this corner of the bush could be opened up for settlement. He began the process by building himself a comfortable lodge. The magistrate was very persuasive and articulate. He was, after all, a classics graduate from Oxford, and successive governments were hoodwinked into putting money into bizarre schemes for settlement along the river. The schemes all failed and when the magistrate went home to die, the government gave up that part of the country. The beautiful rest-house by the river still remained. The local people lived in little shacks in rectangular blocks, with many drains and trenches to try to keep out river water. The people here were an exciting mixture of Warraus and Caribs, traders, bird-catchers, fishermen, failed pork-knockers, and fugitives from more observant authority in town.

Two small boy porters escorted us to the lodge – a thing of beauty, white with a thatched roof, and a veranda all round cool bedrooms with jalousie windows. The old caretaker, Miss T, who made the best bakes in the country, escorted us with great ceremony to our respective rooms where we unpacked and tried to sleep off the effects of the sea. When you come off the water at the landing, your body does not recognise this right away and you feel as if you are still being tossed about. This often lasts for about as long as it takes to do business on the landing by the black water. After some hours, Fred woke me up insisting we go drinking. We left the house and walked to the landing, trying the first clean-looking shop we saw. We went in and sat at the counter. There was no one there to serve us. We tapped, rapped, banged and were ready to leave and try somewhere else when she came out, the sweetest round face and the shapeliest body in the country. Carib, with a hint of Venezuela mestizo.

"Why you not at your counter? You selling or not?" Fred demanded.

"We selling, you can't see is a shop?" she replied in a quiet, almost inaudible whisper.

When I got to know her better, I learnt that Hermina never spoke in anything but an unmoved dry whisper. No amount of turmoil or excitement could cause her to raise her voice or display emotion.

"Come, girl, we want some cold beers," demanded Fred.

"The beer's not cold. The ice finish and none come on the steamer," was the soft reply.

"This is rass," Fred boomed, "we got to find some cold beers today in this hell hole."

"You want the beer or not?" she responded, still with her eyes modestly downcast and her voice soft, with no sign of irritation or reaction.

During this exchange, I was looking past Fred and his ice problems and seeing wide, dark eyes and soft lips, and a neck that looked as if it would feel like simatoo if you passed your fingers over it. I smiled my best one and accepted the offer of lukewarm beer, and tried to roll out some minor flattery. Judging from her expression, I assumed that I was getting nowhere, and ended half in jest, "Why don't you come visit me at the rest-house tonight?"

All she said was, "OK, which is your room?" That was all. Nothing else. Not another sign of interest or inflection of sensuality.

Before leaving, Fred asked, "This your shop?"

"No," she replied, "is my husband's."

I assumed that this was the last of Hermina, especially in light of her last remark. I was in bed at the rest-house, under my mosquito net and on my way to other lands, when I heard a light knock on the door and a soft voice saying, "I could come in?" It occurred to me later that I had not heard the sound of her footsteps before the knock. She came in, walked up to the bed, climbed under the net and sat at my feet. Hermina conducted a brief inquisition in short sentences, checking my age, family, job and whether I was "ticklish", still with no more than her lifeless whisper. Then, in relation to nothing I had done or said, she loosened her hair, pulled her dress over her head and dived under my covering sheet. In bed, she was different; she still made little sound but she was demanding and tigerish. I fell asleep exhausted many hours later and did not hear her leave. When I awoke to find her gone, I did not get back to sleep and morning found me in a haze of weariness, seasickness and disbelief.

I was anxious to boast of my conquest to Fred since he was usually the victor in our match-play over women. At first he did not believe my story and assumed I was delirious from exhaustion, since we did not have much to drink. We went about our duties in some unpleasantness, for I was hurt that he could believe that I would make up a story like that. The reason we were in the area was to organise the people, especially the fishermen, into co-operatives. We must have sounded like fools to them since their ancestors had been living communally for thousands of years, and they were accustomed to owning so many things in common. But co-ops were the buzz at the time and you had to co-operate whether you wanted to or not. I had no intention of telling my chief that the people thought we were wasting their time. We gave them the gaff and signed them all up. At the end of our first day, I suggested we return to the little shop. It took a mock row with Fred, but we agreed to a compromise where I could have a few minutes in the shop and then we would leave in search of a proper shop with ice-cold Banks beer.

It was not a pleasant occasion. Hermina had her son with her, about two years old, and showed no sign or recognition or coyness. Fred tried to be fresh but without raising her voice or her eyes she snapped, "Don't make your eyes and pass me." Then she turned to me and said, "My husband wanted to meet you." I had the involuntary ice down the spine that comes when I get unpleasant surprises. My hands shook a little. "Mr Palmer," she said to the back room, "these are the men who came in yesterday," and she went into the back of the shop. Mr Palmer was a big brown-skinned man. He looked weather-beaten and poorly kept, and came out in a sweaty shirt and with dribble on his chin. He had evidently just awoken. He had a large domed head and a spreading forehead and, when he put on his glasses, gave the impression of someone who might have had distinguished features and aspect in the past. All he was prepared to tell me was that he had a little coconut grant down the river and had recently bought the shop for something to do, and somewhere to be, when he came to the landing. He asked us many insightful questions about our work on the river and offered us more hot beer, this time on the house. He had a suspiciously comfortable grasp of government activity and politics. As we were leaving, he invited us to visit his grant with the assurance that we would leave well-laden with fruit and provisions to take to town. I was in a quandary, for I had no idea if Hermina intended to see me again and if I should expect her.

Fred and I played cards, "rap-bob-a-pool", to while away the rest of the evening. For some hours we played and talked about this and that, chose the national football team, selected a new West Indies captain, rearranged the world, jailed some prominent Comrades, resolved our romantic dilemmas and specified a cabinet reshuffle which focused on the transfer of our minister as ambassador to a distant republic, preferably Afghanistan or Mongolia. Then we came to the topic, Hermina. Fred agreed that she was pretty and wasted on an old wreck like Palmer. He was still sceptical of my claim to Valhalla the previous night and tried to find a way to make his case without hurting my feelings. The door opened quietly and she came in, said goodnight politely and said to me in her emotionless whisper, "I can't stay long tonight, the boy sick." As I walked with her to my room, I looked back to see Fred staring at me in utter amazement, his eyes and mouth wide open, his cards still in his hand.

That night before she left, she suggested that I go to the shop next evening since Mr Palmer was not going to be there and she was afraid to be seen sneaking out late every night. I agreed without thinking, heedless of a jocular warning from Fred that I was getting reckless.

The next night found me in a little bed in the back room of the shop. I promised her everything. I was going to come back for her and rescue her from the miserable old man. I was going to carry her to America and give her a car and buy her new clothes and mind her son. I handed her all the money I had with me, mine plus the Ministry's allowances for the trip. She did not react, only a half smile betrayed that she heard my frantic promises. Suddenly, we were interrupted by the sounds of a heavy man crossing the plank across the trench and opening the front door of the shop. Then came the voice of Palmer calling for Hermina. I recalled that the farmers here always carried their shotguns. I did not know that it was possible to get a severe headache so fast. I lost all interest in women, love or beauty in any shape or form. All Hermina said in her dry whisper was, "I think Mr Palmer came back home. You better go through the window."

I scrambled through the window, trousers and shirt in hand, dropped heavily to the ground and ran into a trench filled with mud, stinking and oozy. I recovered my senses enough to remain quiet in the mud for a few minutes to allow Palmer to settle down. Then, having recovered my breath and put on my clothes, I crawled through the dark, guessing my way to the rest-house. I limped my stinking self into the bathroom to get the mud and the smell off me. Fred came out to help me with the mud on Miss T's well-scrubbed kitchen floor, but could not help laughing in fits for minutes at an end.

I did not go back to the black river on the next trip, Lennox went instead. Of course they tortured me when they came back to the office a week later and talked about everything else except what I wanted to know. Eventually, I grabbed Fred by his shirtjac and demanded news of my angel.

"Did you see Hermina? Did you go to the shop? Did she ask for me?"

"Oh," Fred grinned, "they say she gone to Venezuela."

Big Joe

BIG Joe was my hero as a little boy. He had a marvellous range of skills and careers. For much of my life I wanted to be like Big Joe, though my granny disapproved of my low ambitions. For starters, Joe was the village crier. Early in the morning, Joe would pass on his big Raleigh bike with one brake and no fenders, a tawa dangling from the crossbar. Every fifty yards, he would whack the tawa with a hammer and announce the latest news, usually a death: "ALERTHA BENJAMIN OF PIKE STREET IS DEAD. FUNERAL THIS AFTERNOON AT HALF PAST FOUR. SHE GOING TO BURY AT KITTY GROUND."

Then he would give it another whack. BANGGGG!

Sometimes he cycled through so fast that you could miss the details of the announcement, but Joe was not fussy; he gave additional or repeat information in a less official voice if asked. Then another bang and the full announcement again.

"Who dead, Joe?"

"Cousin Lertha, from Pike Street."

BANGGGGG!

"ALERTHA BENJAMIN OF PIKE STREET IS DEAD ... ."

Joe caused me to receive my first lesson in modern languages. Once he announced of a dead villager: "SHE GOING TO BURY AT LAPANTEAR." My granny had to explain that he was referring to Le Repentir, the big burial ground in Georgetown.

Sometimes the village council found itself in serious financial difficulties, unable to pay the rubbish-collectors and drain-diggers. Joe would then be commissioned to make a different cry: "PAY UP YOUR RATES. DON'T LET THE BAILIFF HAVE TO VISIT YOU. PAY UP YOUR RATES."

This was usually sandwiched by irreverent comments on the members of the village council.

Joe had the big voice necessary for getting your attention early in the morning. It was deep and resonant. You could not claim not to have heard when Joe passed through.

Joe was also the grave-digger. When you got to a burial ground, be it Anglican, Methodist, General, Hindu or Muslim, Joe and his assistant would be leaning under the nearest tree. Having dug the six foot hole, he would wait with his planks and ropes to lower the coffin into the ground.

During the last rites, he would squat under the tree drinking from a half bottle of high-wine. When the newfangled idea of concrete tombs came into being, he adapted to the new technology and would have your tomb built with one end open. He was always very efficient for I calculated that by the third verse of "What A Friend We Have in Jesus", you were well sealed in the tomb.

Joe did not work at all funerals for there were some big shots who had their relatives buried from funeral parlours in town and had no need for the services of a local. He held no grudges, for he would still attend if he at all knew the deceased, and would arrive dressed in his formal outfit; perfectly pressed black suit, white shirt, stiff and starched with a wing collar, and a black bow tie but no shoes. Since he was very tall and very dark, he never failed to attract attention in the crowd outside the church. He made me think of great warrior princes of the old country. When on grave-digging duty, you could not help but marvel at his strength and the hard sculpture of his forearms and shoulders. He was immensely strong and demonstrated his powers whenever there was a crisis in the village requiring brute physical force, like somebody's horse or donkey stuck in mud or a house fallen off its blocks.

Joe was a drummer. Not a drummer in a band or in the military. Joe was a tassa drummer. There was no Indian drummer who could play the drums as sweetly as he did, and all the Hindus in the village agreed. Any "dutty" digging ceremony before a wedding or any other celebration was incomplete without Joe and his tassa filling the night with his intricate rhythms. The sight of Joe and his drums leading a crowd of middle-aged Indian ladies on their ceremonial march is one of the mysterious memories of my youth. He was of course always present at Hindu weddings, and when the danceman began his moves they would transport each other in a frenzy of ecstasy as the music and the rhythm raced each other. It is fortunate that these weddings were always well supplied in old BG, for Joe was a big eater.

I asked my granny about Joe and she gave snatches of his story. He had been a pork-knocker and then captain of one of the most successful crews to hit Imbaimadai. Like many of the breed, he had long since lost his earnings. He had also been a Santapee, one of the bands of young toughs who had wreaked havoc with their violence and arrogance before the war. It was even rumoured that he was a member of Freddy Bandoola's notorious gang. Granny assured me that this was the first time that white people walked in fear. Even she, so totally steeped in Anglican piety, had a glow in her eyes whenever she talked of those times. Joe was also a champion stick-fighter and seemed destined for greatness before the government cracked down on the bands and brought jail and ruination on rebels.

At Christmas, Joe and some of his old gang would come together to play masquerade. Joe could beat the "kittle" drum as well as he could beat the tassa, and on the days before Christmas he would lead his boys with the young flouncers, the Mother Sally and the mad bull from street to street. Joe would go by, his long head at an angle and his jaw jutting forward, his eyes looking at some distant inspiration. I wish I knew what had made him so proud and regal. I wish I'd had a chance to ask him about the days of the Santapee and the deeds of Freddy Bandoola, and his days on the Potaro and the gold he had found, and the women he had known and the fights he had won and the times he had come close to death. All I was able to do was admire the man as he led the band through our lane with the drums rippling and the flouncers swooping for the offerings we threw from our front windows.

I did not think that the big man was aware of my existence at all. As for myself, I grew older and was sent to the big school in town in preparation to become a lawyer or doctor, and lost interest in the affairs and personalities of our village. I hated school and the mimicry of Englishmen, and pretentious red people and tortured frustrated Blacks and Indians. I wanted nothing that the life in BG offered me and I was aware that my performance in the big school was neither what my grandparents expected nor what I knew I was capable of. But I had no interest in becoming like all the others, licking the boots of the second-rate bores who ran our colony, and I did not think that playing cricket and talking nonsense made me any better. I came home from school for my Easter holidays and to my granny's disgust was now a drinker of beer and a smoker, and used all the words my family abhorred. We had an argument about my downward path and I stormed out of the house in anger and to avoid seeing Granny cry.

I hung around the market for a while that night, had a few and tried to figure ways out of my dilemma. Distraction offered itself, however, in the person of Julie, a girl who had been in my class in the village school. In the interim, she had become one of the hot girls in the village and she was still pretty enough, though the effects of her force-ripeness were beginning to show. I got the conversation going and thought that I could have some fun, as she seemed fascinated by my chatter and new-found manliness. I proposed a walk to the sea walls and she consented. On our way to the walls, one of her men intercepted us and in the ensuing argument, a fight started. I was a great fighter in school but there was no way I could hold out against one of the village toughs.

I made a great defence but was inwardly prepared for the licking of my life. A small crowd gathered, the men shouting "Heh!" to punctuate each blow I received, and the women giving generous advice on tactics. I was having the worst of it and as I fell to the ground, I heard a loud shout and felt a strong hand grip my shoulders. My assailant was pulled off me at the same time. It was Big Joe.

He shook me roughly and proceeded to address me by my grandfather's name. "Mr Stanley, what you doing on the road and why you tangling with this no-good gal?" He ignored the rest of the group and gave me a lecture that sounded suspiciously like my grandfather's, without the pompous English and with some bushman's curses attached. I heard all over again that I was destined to become a great lawyer or a doctor and bring glory to the village and honour to my aging granny. I did not realise before this that Big Joe even knew who I was, never mind that he expected me to live out dreams for him and the rest of the village. He who had been my childhood idol, my symbol of manliness, was brutally and crudely clear that the hopes of people like him rested on me and what I achieved at the big school. It certainly did not include fights over the likes of Julie.

I have never been able to admit to my grandparents or my aunts that Big Joe was the real reason I took to my books and battled through the college and made myself successful amongst the bourgeois in this colony. They would be hurt and dismayed, for they believe the story I usually tell on public occasions held in my honour, that I owe it all to them.

Bourda

I T was only last Saturday that we agreed to come to the test match on Easter Monday. "We" meant three of us; Baps, Bingie and I. We worked it out that since play started at eleven, and the gates were often closed by nine o'clock, we would have to start queuing by six-thirty in the morning. This created serious problems since that meant leaving home by five-thirty. The preparation of the food we would need for our day's nourishment would need to start on Easter Sunday night.

Negotiations for the food added complications to each of our domestic lives. Baps was married but was not on very good terms with his wife since he had returned home from his last job. He had got himself involved with a plump young girl while in the bush and word of his indiscretions had seeped all the way back to the coast. His wife had raised bloody hell over the story and suspected, quite rightly as it happened, that the young woman had made substantial inroads into the money Baps had earned on the project. He has had to make numerous promises and compromises to restore normal relations.

Bingie is not married, he is "living home" with a country girl he met last year. One Saturday night, he slapped her around because she had cursed him and refused to cook for us when we had assembled at his house drunk. After the first few slaps, she had run to the kitchen for the chopper, threatening to cut off his right hand. Bingie had to back off and apologise. We had to restrain Betty from getting us all into trouble with the police.

I am a bachelor and I still live at Ma's house. She and I are at war over remarks she made from the kitchen when Dolly was last by our yard. Dolly is not pretty, I know, but she is a good girl, easy to please and quite content with the sporadic attention I am able to give. There was no reason, however, for Ma to call her a "foffie-eyed wretch". Sometimes I believe if even Shakira herself were to visit, Ma would find something mean to say about her.

In our crowd, you cannot arrive at Bourda without a basket full of food and drink. That is how you convince your friends and admirers that you have your womenfolk under control. To sustain this masquerade, we made demeaning compromises. Poor Baps may never be able to see his fat girl again. Bingie had to promise many gifts and jewellery. I suspect, though, that the women all recognised that their own reputations were on the line if any of us were to arrive at the ground with a less than perfect lunch kit. So five-thirty Easter Monday morning found us at the Pike Street bus stop waiting for the first Kitty/Regent, each with a basket and numerous other bags and appendages. I had my mother's best ice-flask and several bottles of Coke, in addition to chow mein, fowl curry, rice, patties, pine tarts, half a sponge cake, two plates, two spoons and four plastic cups. Bingie and Baps brought the rum, two large bottles each, in addition to food. I was not allowed to keep rum in the house since my mother had joined the revival group last year.

Getting on the bus was another story. The old Motor Transport buses had narrow turnstiles that made entry with two or three bags per person a hazardous business. Since most of the other passengers were also on their way to cricket there was much good-natured badinage, and eventually we helped each other, passing bags, baskets and even one or two small boys over the turnstiles to get things going. We reached the North Road gates at six o'clock to find Bourda already alive. There were hundreds of die-hards already in line, and fellows from the country who had come down by train from Berbice for the weekend and were camping out in the open on the grassy stretch on the North Road. The out-of-town guys had used up all their cooked rations by this time and were buying food at cut-throat prices from the city food vendors, always on the ready to cash in on a good thing.

Some of the country boys were in a sorry state. Many had come by train since Friday night to see the great local hero Rohan Kanhai make a big score. Kanhai had made a majestic 89 on the first day and, though he had not got to his century, it was clear to all concerned that at his second go on Saturday he would pulverise the Australian bowlers and make his first century in a home test. Many of the boys had come laden with food, money, drink and high expectations of a good time. Kanhai was the first master batsman of Indian descent in the West Indies team, so he generated special reverence from people of his own background, especially those from the sugar estate villages from which stars like Kanhai had been recruited. Unfortunately, before a roaring crowd on Saturday, an Australian fast bowler named Hawke found the ball of his life, completely defeated the local hero and bowled him out. The crowd went as quiet as if it was church.

Many of the fans were in a dilemma; their hero was out and would not have a chance to redeem himself. Why bother to stay? Some had spent most of their money and not a few were without the ready to afford the train trip back home. Many had bet huge sums with speculating Georgetown fans on Kanhai's hundred, and had had to pay up when he was defeated. They hung about squatting on the grass, their new shirts and picnic clothes now bedraggled, and their unshaved, unwashed faces highlighting their pitiful stories.

We joined the queue for the Northwest stand since it was covered and since a large number of our drinking buddies and fellow cricket arguers were going to be there. Those who got there first tried to preserve some room for those further back in the line. This was possible because "Mammy Eye" was counted as one of our gang and had long since been deemed a "rogue and a vagabond" by the city magistrates for persistent assault, battery, and "resisting a peace officer in the carrying out of his duties". Anyone trying to get a seat in our corner was frightened off by his growl, and by the advice of people knowledgeable about crime and vagabondage in Kitty and environs. We joined the queue about half a mile down the road and as we inched forward the morning sun rose in our faces, reminding us how long we had been awake.

Queues are jolly at Bourda. Preliminary arguments begin about the blindness of the selectors, the arrogance of the cricket board of control, players selected who should not have been and forgotten players who should have been. Controversy was also generated because a local writer had suggested that Nurse, the Barbadian, had not earned his place and that Cornelius, the local boy, should have played in his stead. Since Nurse was my favourite player at the time I could not let this go unanswered, but since I am short, thin and bespectacled, and without the necessary loud voice that helps in these quarrels, I was shouted down. My lack of patriotism was denounced by several large and voluble die-hards, and Baps and Bingie had to save me from myself despite their disgust at my open heresy.

The talk then drifted to the local officials who had made fools of themselves by refusing to allow our leading umpire into the stands because the local umpires were on strike. Unfortunately for them, when the Prime Minister arrived at the game on the first day, he had joined the umpire in the bleachers, where they sat on a soft drink case together, and the resulting publicity put the board in a bad light. They had no defenders in the North Road queue.

By the time we got to the bridge over the canal the queue started to disintegrate, since latecomers from the Scheme walked straight to the head of the line and tried to muscle their way in. Early birds such as ourselves from Campbelville, Lodge and Kitty were not going to allow these hooligans to do us out of our hard-won seniority, and eventually the pushing match threatened to become ugly. The lone policeman on duty could do nothing about it and looked away until a few guys fell off the end of the bridge into the canal. This sobered everyone down a bit, though some unfortunates lost their lunches and spent the day looking bad and smelling worse.

We got into the ground about eight-thirty and wove our way through the crowded wooden stand to the gang in "our" corner. Even though it was over two hours to start of play the stand was almost full and the gates were closed about half an hour after we got in. The trouble with getting up so early to watch cricket is that by the time you get to a seat, you are already hungry and thirsty so you have to open the food, start eating, open the rum and start the drinking. This is also advised if your lady made mistakes about the time it would take before your food went off. One fellow opened his chow mein at lunchtime only to find it had expired some time before.

You cannot eat alone at cricket. You have to pass your bowl, flask, cake-tin and anything else around your friends. Your friends would have brought friends and would pass your fried rice or roti to them. Of course, a friend of friends will pass you some of their food. Flask and bowl covers were pressed into service when plates ran out. The drinking was even more serious. Each large bottle is ceremoniously produced, the seal is broken and a few drops are sprinkled or thrown over the shoulder to appease the spirits. The drinking commences. Muddy, a loud-mouthed accountant in the civil service, had walked with a bottle of scotch that he had brought to impress the gang. Unfortunately, he passed his bottle around before taking a drink himself, and by the time it returned to him there was only a tiny drop to be squeezed out. Muddy began to recoup his losses by making major inroads into any bottle passed to him. By ten o'clock, Muddy was drunk and fast asleep. I do not believe he saw a single ball played even though he remains an authority on the events of that day.

You have a lot of time to waste before the game starts. You could watch the players warm up in front of the pavilion. You could try to guess the names of the visiting team, quite a feat since they all looked alike. You could stare at the signs encouraging you to drink Russian Bear Rum and rub with Canadian Healing Oil. You could stare at the trees rising over the tops of the stands and admire the birdmen perched high on the Regent Street side. You could eat again or vary your diet by getting boiled channa from Channaman or boiled corn from Beaks. Channaman was expert at throwing his parcels to his patrons no matter how high up. By game time we were so bored we applauded everything. The groundsman putting in the stumps, the umpires walking out, the drunk who managed to get on the field and give the police a good run around. You could look up in the pavilion and wonder at the big shots watching cricket in dark suits and ties.

By the time the day really got started, we were bored enough to get into pointless arguments and ridiculous bets. What a day it was. I made a bet about Nurse with a large red-skinned guy from Buxton. Nurse promptly got out first ball. Then Sobers came in and started to hit the Australian bowlers all over Bourda. Bets about the great man began to fly and Bingie bet a guy from Courantyne that "Sobers will fifty". As Sobers approached the half century mark, Bingie, now under the cloud of rum, scotch and overeating, became abusive and insulting to an equally drunk Berbician. On the brink of his fifty, Sobers got out and Bingie refused to pay up. The gang turned on him and in the ensuing scuffle, my glasses and my mother's favourite ice-flask were broken. Bingie did not learn. When the Australians began their second innings, he started an argument with everybody because Sobers was opening the bowling from the top end instead of Hall. He claimed that the skipper was a selfish "pro" and a brainless captain. This enraged the whole collection of drunks, including complete strangers who attached themselves to our well-fed and watered company. When Simpson the Australian captain and opening batsman clouted Sobers for a four, Bingie made large bets waving the entire contents of his pocket in reckless abandon. Sobers promptly bowled Simpson two balls later, knocking the stumps out of the ground in spectacular fashion. Bingie could not pay all his creditors and almost had to give up his shirt to a big fellow from Mackenzie who was late in the queue to collect his winnings.

As the day grew hotter and the hard greenheart stand began to hurt our backsides, and the cramped postures in which we were crouched began to take effect, cricket watching became hard work. Everyone had to stand and stretch in between overs and during water breaks to keep off cramp and stiffness. The standing break took longer and longer until the crowd waited till the bowler was running in for the first ball to sit down. Also the sun now beat straight into our faces, unlike the faces of the big shots in the pavilion and the rich people in Flagstaff stand. And we were drunk and tired and sleepy. The cricket was fascinating that day but most of us were tired out by liquor, loud arguments and the heat of the sun, and so missed all the subtleties of a masterly display by the spin bowler Gibbs. As he wove confusion amongst the Australian batsmen, we were too beaten up to appreciate the subtle arts of the Guianese master. Australia was routed.

But so are we. We are walking home elated but tired and sore. We have
to walk since there is no chance that there will be any room on the bus.
Baps has spent the money he promised his wife and Bingie has no hope of
getting his madam her bangles for some time. And me, I have to explain to
Ma about her special ice-flask.

Choker

T HREE vendors passed down Wilfred Street on Saturday mornings. First of all Knotty the kerosene oil vendor on a three-wheeled truck with one large front wheel and two normal-sized rear wheels. Knotty was short for Knotty Goady and referred to his prominent hernia. You had to stand in the cab to drive the truck, which was very convenient for Knotty, who had grave difficulties sitting. It was my job as the boy in the house to buy one and a half gallons of oil from Knotty.

Second came Babyshrimps, who was a fish vendor. Her tiny wizened husband pushed a two-wheeled handcart on which was placed a tray of the fish, shrimp and other seafood which she purveyed. Babyshrimps had a delightful call, the long "SHIRIIIIIIIIMPSandfish!" The "fish" at the end was often lost in the dying notes of the phrase. Babyshrimps was a fat and cheerful woman who greeted everyone as she passed through the street, stopping to receive or impart new gossip and generally comment on the state of affairs in the village. Since my grandmother was an extremely stuffy and mannerly person who was a great believer in not mixing and meddling, I was always surprised at the warmth of the greetings exchanged with Babyshrimps. Babyshrimps was lewd and loud and raucous, all the sins that Granny attempted to beat out of me and especially my sisters. One of her maxims was an amendment of the poster that decorated the school wall. "Quiet speech is a mark of refinement, noisy speech is the mark of a fisherwoman." Yet she greeted Babyshrimps warmly, and though the jokes exchanged were less funny and untainted by references to reproductive functions, they were jokes all the same. Baby always wiped her hands when calling out to Granny and called her Mistress, in a most ingratiating way. Granny never bought any shrimps from her to my recollection.

Then came Choker the ice vendor. There was no compromise in the case of Choker. Granny loathed Choker with a passion. She would make the most pained of faces when he passed by, leading his emaciated donkey pulling his rickety donkey cart. It was the same face she made when the cat made a mess under the bed and the offending spot could not be found, and when yawaries killed her prized Creole fowl cock. Choker had blocks of ice covered in sugar bags from which he chipped portions for one cent or a penny. You went with a bowl to buy your ice, though the Warington family, who had no manners or training, bought their penny ice and carried it home in their hands. Choker was very fond of Granny. He never failed to greet her if she was near the front landing as he passed, and she never failed to huff and sniff and make disgusted faces.

Choker was one of the village disgraces. Some years before I was born, he had been a cabinet-maker during the day and a musician at night. He went home from a gig too late to identify the man fleeing his mistress's bedroom. Choker had gone in search of his suspect and poured a bottle of acid in a fellow's face, badly disfiguring him for life. Unfortunately for Choker, he had attacked the wrong man, fixing upon the only one of his friends who had not participated in his lady's largesse. He was arrested and convicted, the judge sentencing him to a long prison term and twelve strokes with the cat-o'-nine-tails. He emerged from jail badly broken and the most dishevelled human being of my childhood memory. He was never tidy or clean on any occasion. Even Buttors the noted fowl thief, and Angel Gabriel the village drunk, could muster clean dark suits for weddings and funerals, and Big Foot Colleen had a church dress for Easter and for selling food at the Methodist fellowship tea. Choker was always dirty, his shirt was always in tatters, his pants were always a few inches from arrest for indecent exposure, and he had grey stubble that never became a proper beard. He also limped badly when he descended from the cart to sell his ice.

Once, Choker was riding his cart through our street and a big shot was going in the opposite direction, the two meeting at a narrow section outside our house. The driver, obviously a man of great importance, refused to reverse to a convenient spot to let Choker through and Choker stood his ground. There was a deep trench and gutter on either side. We feared that Choker might curse the driver or even become violent. Choker took decisive action. He placed the reins of his donkey on the cart, alighted and headed for the shade of a nearby genip tree. He sat down under the tree, took out a battered Lighthouse cigarette and lit up. The big shot, pompous and brown-skinned, soon realised that Choker cared not for the ice wasting away in his cart nor for the passage of time. He presumably had important meetings in his bank or commission agency, and soon realized his mistake. He tried to rally support from nearby unlookers, but even Granny was fully behind Choker after an hour. Eventually, he had to reverse in defeat and allow Choker through.

Ice-selling was a dying trade for, in a few years, a few people in the street were able to acquire new "Frigidaires". They went into business. Penny for a whole tray of ice, cent for a half tray. They also sold "flutie", made with sugar and red colouring, for a cent, and "custard block", made with heaven knows what, for a penny. We no longer needed Choker's ice, and when his donkey died he was forced to abandon the business. Choker started a cake shop. A cake shop was one step below a grocery. Bread and cakes in a glass case, sweets and biscuits in large bottles, and lots and lots of sweet drinks. Choker also sold mauby made by his madam, cent- and penny-sized glasses, and a concoction called pine that was red and sweet and variable in taste. Choker had a choice location at the corner of Greenville and Bell Street and should have made a lot of money. I certainly took every opportunity to get a glass of his mauby whenever I had change in my pocket. Hiding in the dark corner behind the door, I would get a whole snack for less than five cents. The thought that Granny disapproved not only of Choker's morals but was aghast that anyone as dirty as he should handle other people's food, made the illicit snacks sweeter. Some traitor in the village reported one of my sneak lunches and I got a good beating from my father, who was in from the bush paying us one of his infrequent visits. I doubt my father had any strong feelings about Choker's hygiene. He had to beat me to keep my granny content with taking care of his children in his absence. Most villagers probably felt like Granny and, in spite of Choker's woman being civilised and reasonably clean, his shop was a place of last resort.

One of the reasons for this was that Choker became increasingly erratic in its operation. He often refused to open his shop on rainy or cloudy days. He also closed his shop if there was horse racing at D'urban Park, when he spent all day dirty and dishevelled at the track. He then began getting into arguments with his suppliers, and especially the bakers. Some were never paid. They could not find Choker for deliveries. The supplier of local sweets had a row with Choker's mistress and refused to sell them any more, robbing them of valuable trade in hasserback, jujubes, butter sticks and sourdrops.

Choker became a taxi driver. He acquired a beaten and well-worn Morris Oxford, which he used to ply the route to Georgetown. Choker faced many disadvantages for taxi-driving. His lapses in personal hygiene made life in the front seat near the driver very unpleasant. The taxi itself was always liable to collapse with an overheating radiator, or some other catastrophe, in the middle of Long Road. Choker would then go to the canal with a bucket to find water to bring his car back to life. Then there was the problem of tyres. Choker collected them after other taxi drivers had discarded them as unsafe, and you were very likely to spend part of your journey waiting in a vulcanising shop, or by the side of some road in the rain, while Choker coped with another blow-out.

Choker always got business, however. Taxis were always hard to get in town, and if you were late for work or school he was very often the only hope in a crisis, tyres and engine permitting. He had the quality that he did not discriminate against any passenger on the grounds of race, size or destination. People who wanted out-of-the-way routes knew that Choker would accept any request. It was not unknown, however, for Choker to take passengers through such disparate parts of the city that some of the passengers would become angry at being taken on a round-the-town ride and start rows, and eventually leave the taxi. One timid passenger, afraid of Choker's reputation and unwilling to complain, ended up on the east coast six miles from home. At rush hour, Choker could not find it in his heart to refuse any passengers. He would leave the terminus full and still stop for new passengers. All were welcome. Very often, the old passengers would be leaving from the other door as he kept bringing new passengers in along the way.

The even tenor of life in our community was severely disrupted when Choker got religious. He announced to his passengers that he found God one night whilst listening to a sermon by an itinerant evangelist preaching at the market square in town, that he became convinced that he needed salvation and was now a firm believer in the Gospel. He acquired a large battered bible and proceeded to read it avidly when taxi business was slow, or indeed when he did not feel like driving. Choker's apparent conversion from wickedness threw the village into some turmoil, for his about-face disturbed all the certainties by which we classified people. Unfortunately, Choker was serious about his new found faith and presented himself along with his huge bible at church. My grandmother almost fainted with shock, and the plight of Mrs Nutting, a respected and prim matriarch of one of society's notable light-skinned families, was the talking point for weeks. Choker joined her pew near the front and the good lady's discomfiture and humiliation drew sympathy or amusement. The vicar wasted no time and, even before Mrs Nutting had complained, he bearded Choker with a long and complicated harangue about communicants and catechism and standards that made no sense, and became more convoluted as the vicar went on. The vicar was not a man of great intelligence or learning and, though most of his parish did not perceive it, he had not developed very much from the clerkship in a store from which he had fled – via a very short and limited divinity course – to be a missionary in Demerara. He found, however, that the more educated and sophisticated parishioners, the teachers and business people who had been to England, were openly contemptuous of him. His argument with Choker did not add to his dignity or his prestige, and he felt that at the end of the confrontation he had lost much ground.

Choker had not heard of the Reformation or the troubles of Henry VIII, so the next week he presented himself at St Mary's Roman Catholic Church, still clasping his formidable bible. Choker's reception there was at least more efficient. He was shepherded to a quiet corner, where he could do the least harm, and instructed by the priest that he needed to do many things to himself before he came back.

Choker decided that he had better go to the Methodist chapel, where at least he knew some of the people. He lasted there for many weeks for no one in the chapel had the slightest idea what could be done to cope with this menace. And he was a menace. Choker slept through most of the liturgy and all of the hymn singing. When he did come to life, he would read ostentatiously from his bible and was very surprised that no one else found time to look into that delightful volume. He also had a habit of asking questions, usually intelligent ones to which no one, least of all the beleaguered lay preachers, knew the answers. His outrageous presence was tolerated on local preacher Sundays, but on parson Sundays the good folk were severely embarrassed. Eventually Sister Bentham, one of those dreaded matriarchs who frequently boast of their willingness to be rude and personal in pursuit of speaking the truth, tackled Choker and gave specific advice about baths, clothes, haircuts and silence in the house of the Lord. Choker by this time was so well versed that he was able to rebut her arguments in his blunt style, lacing his responses with many inappropriately applied texts, generally from the early books of the Old Testament.

On parson Sunday, despite the best hopes of the faithful, Choker interrupted the parson's homily to ask for further explanations. The parson tried to deal with the matter in a broad-minded way and suggested that he would be happy to discuss matters at the end of the service. Choker accepted this and all would have gone well, for the Methodist preacher felt in his thoughtful moments that there was something vaguely Christian about welcoming the village ruffian to feast with the faithful of his congregation. But the complaints about Choker came fast and furious. A delegation of the leaders took the bus to discuss the matter in the minister's office and the minister, a timorous though godly soul, wavered between his conscience and his hypocrites, afraid to take a decision.

The matter could have become very nasty but for the intervention of the Bible Holiness Gospel Mission, which had recently emerged in temporary quarters in the school hall. At first this was a happy move for Choker. Bible Holiness was a "clap hand" church, much given to happy and extended singing of lively tunes from the American South. Choker did not sleep. In fact Choker retrieved his battered saxophone, long silent since his pre-prison years, and was eagerly welcomed as part of the holy jollification. And they all carried bibles. Choker and his battered bible were not so odd in this house. There were problems, however. The Bible Mission encouraged testifying, especially about the sins and wickedness from which you were saved and for which salvation you were therefore grateful. Choker joined in this practice enthusiastically. Unfortunately, since his resumé included genuine rapine, mayhem and rascality, and since his recollections were not sanitised, they brought many of the serious saints to fainting. Though if truth be told, it provided great entertainment for the younger and less mature of the men and boys. Nevertheless, Choker and his saxophone became a regular feature, and his "specials" given at the commencement of each night of the crusade, conducted by an evangelist from Wichita, were the talk of the village. His version of "What a friend" had many weak souls tapping their feet, shaking their heads and sometimes even much worse.

It all looked positive, and at least no one told him about his dirty clothes. Unfortunately, on the last night of the crusade, Choker was leaving to go home with his battered sax under his arm when he overheard two of the missionaries sharing a joke about someone. The words "clown" and "smelly" featured prominently. He soon realised they were talking about him and he quickly confronted them, though fortunately they did not understand much of what he said, though I assure you all of it was obscene.

Choker returned to his taxi until it finally expired and he turned to selling newspapers in front of the village market. He became a great arguer, especially on matters of politics and religion, for which his knowledge of the most peculiar quotes from obscure books in the Old Testament was a great weapon. My sister tells me he died recently and was not taken to any church for a funeral service.

Going Home

A t last we could go home.

We could leave this miserable camp and the canvas roof that lets in the afternoon rain, and the sand which retains the noonday heat, and chiggers, and Carrie's terrible food. Sometimes it is tough to accept that we have only been here for twenty-three months, every one of them a painful and brutal memory. Why did I come? It wasn't such a tough decision at the time. A lot of other young men were doing it. It looked very easy. You collected all your savings, you borrowed from your family and friends, you went into the bush and, in a year, you came back rich, able to afford gaberdine and trouserine suits; and to drink White-Horse whiskey, and to go to the races at D'urban Park and place bets on the horses without worrying about your next meal, and walk into the Woodbine with a beautiful red woman in tow. It was easy. Many had done it before. Jacques had come back from Kurupung in a Booker's taxi with money to burn and had thrown out all his household furniture. He instructed his wife to buy everything brand new and had even bought a grand piano – cash – from Psaila's which turned out to be too large for his gallery. So he called in a contractor to make extensive extensions. No one in Jacques' family had any remote interest in playing the piano, or any other musical instrument for that matter, but he reckoned that a piano was what rich white people had in their homes so he was going to have one too.

It was so easy.

"Brother", from over the "trainline" which divides the village, had gone to Arakaka the same year the river dried up, and the boys got a chance to dig for the gold right there on the river bed. Brother loved to tell me of those magical days when hundreds of men each staked out a little square and worked day and night to wash the gold from the river bed sands, before the rains returned and the river resumed her natural course, covering the precious river gravel. The strange thing was that the steam dredge belonging to the Englishmen who had the legal rights for that stretch of river hardly found an ounce, despite their massive and noisy machine which was stranded on the river bottom when it dried up. The river returned but they still did not find gold with their dredge.

Brother had returned to the village laden with money and had promptly renounced his old friends and forsaken his former haunts. He turned to church-going and a pious life but remained rich, loaded with cash, property, and strange tales of the bush and its victims. Getting rich sounded so easy.

I did not notice that some men came back from the bush with the palms of their hands hardened and covered with a dark callous, which never went away. Not the healthy callous from a manly job like carpentry, which I did when I could get work. It was leathery, dark and rough. I did not take enough notice of men who came back gaunt and defeated with hollow, watery eyes, just as poor as when they left the village. I forgot all about those who never came back at all. All I remembered as I tossed in bed before I slept was Jacques and Brother and Bonny, my youngest uncle who came to visit every once in a while and was the darling of my mother and my aunts and all the other women, and always brought gifts or money for everyone, even us small children. It was easy; I had my own luck. That was what I told Rose, my son's mother.

Now we are breaking up camp and packing to go home. We are going without Batson for he died last year just before Christmas from what Skip alleged was a cold in the stomach. In those days we still had stuff like castor oil and bitters and senna pods in the kit, which we supplemented with bush medicine from the Indians on the other side of the mountain, but Batson died anyway. He was not really a very friendly man but was big and strong and was a willing worker who accepted without complaining the tough miserable jobs at the bottom of the pit that no one else wanted. We buried Batson far away from the river and Skip read some lines from a bedraggled Anglican prayer book. Then we all had drinks from our depleted stock of rum and agreed Batto was a good man. Carrie and I sang hymns till we fell asleep.

That was the last time we could afford to get drunk. We worked day in, day out, from dayclean through the blistering heat, till the thunderstorms came. The storms come every day in the mountains, and the river is always black and ugly, and the trees are always dark and full of every form of stinging insect known to man, and monkeys that would steal from the camp and snakes ready to bite, and wild hogs that once razed the camp when we were away at the river. Once I thought I was gone when I touched an electric eel while having a bath. Berry, who is part Patamona, reckons that it was Kanaima, the evil spirit, trying to take me home. We could not find any gold.

When we first arrived here, Skip and I would paddle for a day to the river landing where there was a shop and we could get rations of flour and saltfish and rice at murderous prices. But our money ran out and we had to trust, and eventually we were bargaining away all the gold that we were yet to find until, finally, Uncle Wesley refused us any more trust. Though Skip is big and can be very loud and aggressive, he was unable to move Uncle, fat and benign though he appeared. We paddled back to the camp consumed by anxiety and anger. I dreamed of the day when we would get into our corial, paddle to the landing loaded with dust and nuggets, and drop them in front of Wesley, thus wiping off our debts and claiming sweet revenge. Ah! I dreamed of the look on Uncle's face when we arrived triumphant in the little shack-cum-rumshop-cum-whorehouse from which he reigned.

It is tough working on a stomach rebelling against strange concoctions. Edible game had become harder to find, even if we had ammunition for the hunt. And what work! We worked by the riverside pit shovelling sand and gravel, mixing the stuff with water, making the mixture and shaking the mixture in the battel pan and searching for gold, and sifting the mixture and shovelling the sand and gravel. We could not afford to buy new tools and shovelling dirt with a broken shovel and a rotten spade was like making bricks for Pharaoh.

As I worked, I remembered that we had to face the river once again to go home. We would have to haggle with a crew of boatmen; curly headed bright-eyed "bovianders", reckless men who had no fear of the river or respect for their fellow man. Then we would face the falls, twenty-six of them on this river, the biggest of which was an evil mixture of jagged rocks and white foamy water which claimed at least one boat every season. Before you come to the bush, the river and the falls and the rapids are just tall tales by drunken old men. They have peculiar names like "Fungula" and "Galsitdownbad". But after you have passed though them, over them, around them, and heard the roar and felt the powerlessness and seen death seconds away, you wake up sweating and shivering in the middle of the night and know you were dreaming of the river. Only bundles of gold would make you face that river again. And no one wanted to appear in his home village without the means to flatter his women and impress his enemies.

At night, we would eat Carrie's food and swap stories around the fire, for it got cold in the Pakaraimas. We might comfort ourselves with music. Carrie has a battered mandolin and knows shantos and the old country songs about treacherous lovers and seductions on the back-dam. On Sunday nights he sang Sankeys; rollicking tunes about salvation and the lost sheep and gospel bells. Those who cared to, joined in, or else dreamt of their women and their children and all the fine Christmases they had lost searching for their El Dorado.

After Batson died we found a few ounces of gold dust, but after brief euphoria we realised that if we took what we had to Uncle Wesley, it would not clear our debts at the shop and we would still not be able to get any flour, saltfish, saltbeef or a new set of tools. So we had to start working again but now a new spirit came over the camp. Men began to wonder aloud if Skip, who had control of the dust and kept it hidden, was to be trusted, and young Jones, who had been a lawyer's clerk in town, wanted to make changes to the bargain we had made when we first set out. That was when we had our first fight. The camp changed after that, the Skip was going to kill him but we eventually got them apart. The sour atmosphere never left. The work remained tedious, the food became even more unpalatable and the worst of our characters came to the surface. Aggrey was a school teacher who became tired of his refined poverty and, though he surprised us with the speed with which he adapted to the work and the physical hardship, he gave the impression that he was meant for better things and was unfortunate to be cast in the company of us peasants. He did most of his damage by sidling up to individuals and cranking them up against Skip and against me, Skip's chosen lieutenant. The worse the food became, and the more boring and pointless the digging and washing seemed, the more he encouraged us to blame Skip or someone else for our sorrows.

My hands have been blistered several times in these twenty-three months and I was too proud to stop working. That would look bad. It would have shown me to be less of a man. So it was with all the first-timers on the crew. I developed sores from the insect bites. My face had become thin and we all became black, really black. Not until you have been baked by this bush sun do you know what black skin is.

The last quarrel was really frightening. Several crew members snapped and the shouting got to talk of killing and cutting off heads. The grumblers blamed Skip and Carrie and me. Some spoke with passion of going home. Finally Skip, who had been quietly brooding during all this carry-on, suddenly got up from the fire and faced down the rebels one by one. He cowed them back into submission and dared anyone who wanted to leave to do it immediately. No one was going anywhere. Who wanted to face the black river and the chance that Kanaima, the evil spirit, would take them? Who was able to afford to hire a boat to get to Bartica? Who was ready to face the humiliation of going back home to face our creditors broke, broken and defeated? That was a bitter night. Mercifully, Carrie refused to sing. No one slept well and we ate the morning concoctions which Carrie called porridge and tea with bitterness in our heart and pain in our eyes.

It was Jones who saw the first nugget. Skip confirmed the find. Then we got another and larger one. Then Skip came up on ounces of dust as he worked the battel pans and the mercury. For four feverish days, the fates of prosperity smiled on their forgotten sons as all our dreams and sufferings seemed suddenly to make sense. Skip weighed our takings and salted them away. By his reckoning we had more than enough to pay our debts and return to civilisation men of substance. We had enough to give Batson's wife her share and make the triumphal entry to the village which we had all been dreaming of. Skip wanted us to be patient. He reckoned we had found a rich one and could make more if we worked the gravel for a few more weeks. This time, however, he was overruled. We had all had enough of bad food and bush fish and bush plants and no women and no drink, and we had suffered two Christmases in this godforsaken stretch of this ugly black river. We were going home. Eventually, Skip had to concede. We would break camp and go home. He would go to Uncle and arrange for the first boat from Bartica to reach Wesley's landing to take us down the river to civilisation.

Skip had left us by the fire to have a pee at the edge of the camp when we heard him scream. We ran to him and saw him squatting on the ground clutching his ankle. We knew, even the first-timers, without asking questions. Bushmaster. We had all heard the old-timers tell the stories of the longest and deadliest snake in the bush. He must have stepped on the creature as he walked in the dark and she had delivered her massive dose of lethal venom. I have heard tell of bad snakes in other parts of the world but they cannot be worse than the Bushmaster. Skip went quickly, he was in horrible pain and his legs and his body turned strange colours. He groaned and screamed and then, mercifully, he became unconscious and died in a few hours near to our dying fire. Early next morning, we buried him next to Batson. Aggrey read the prayers from Skip's prayer book. We all agreed that Skip's wife should get his share of the gold and I was deputised to go to Uncle and make arrangements for a boat to take us to Bartica where we could catch the river ferry for the trip to Georgetown.

We dream of the arrival home. Of walking through the market well dressed in expensive clothes and giving out five-dollar bills to poor relations. Of handing our wives and mothers piles of crisp new notes. Of walking into Fogarty's and saying, "Only the best, never mind the price."

We do not think of the riverboat trip, for some of us can't swim and there are twenty-six falls in the river before we get to Bartica.

Photographs

I found these photographs the other day, old photos from an outing we had when we were in sixth Standard. We posed for our class teacher and I did not even remember that he had given us each a couple of prints. As you can see, this was in the days before colour photography, and when we wore short pants even in big size classes. The girls had to wear Panama hats or berets in the school colour.

I look so strange in that photo. I am the short fat one with the big eyes and flat nose that is the trademark of our family. My nickname at home was Chubby, affectionate but accurate. My nickname in school, however, was not so pleasant. I was not a popular boy and was never the leader in the crowd. The real leader in our crowd was Bobby, the one in front, posing with a big grin and hands on his hips. He was the star of the class; the one the teachers said was born to lead. The footballer, the star athlete, the "sweet boy". The good-looking one, the expert on Bud Abbott and Lone Ranger and Tonto movies. He was the first boy in the class to have a girlfriend and gave Annie a balloon and a doll for Christmas. She gave him a little car and a balloon in return. I do not know what else boyfriends and girlfriends did in those days. I, who was fat and shy and could not run and threw like a girl, tried to be a friend of Bobby's but he did not need me as I added nothing to his image. When he recognised that I needed him and would do anything to be seen in his company he borrowed my pocket money, which he never returned, and got me to buy him popsicles and fudgicles and custard blocks in return for his grudging tolerance of my presence, when it was not too burdensome.

Everyone wanted to be like Bobby and all the other guys looked up to him and tried to wear their clothes like he did. He was the leader in all fashion trends, introducing the fancy haircuts like the Jackson, the flat top, the muff, the Presley, and sweet-boy fads like the cheesecloth kerchief and the turned up collar. At school parties, he was the centre of attention for he could dance extremely well and all the girls wanted to dance with him. Since no one wanted to dance with me and I was afraid to ask, I used to go home from these occasions envious and bitter and wondering why God put some people on earth knowing how to do everything, get all the attention and have all the fun. Bobby went on to try his hand at a number of trades but never succeeded at any of them. He lived with a woman who gave him such a tough time that he beat her senseless and was sent to jail for several years. Eventually, he migrated to England and fell in with a white woman of indeterminate age and occupation who abandoned him to die of pneumonia one winter in a dingy basement in Brixton.

The other popular guy in our class was Roger, the one in the fancy shirt on the right. Roger was popular because he was cute and was the principal's son and had lived for a while in London, was brown skinned, had a posh accent, knew many dirty jokes and introduced us to sex. Perhaps I should explain that some of us knew very little about human biology, whereas Roger spoke with authority backed by claims of experience. Roger attracted the more sophisticated of the class, the better off and lighter-skinned, and those who felt that associating with him could improve their chances of good treatment in school. I could not hope to aspire to be part of his gang since I had none of the passports necessary for entry. I had neither looks nor colour nor notoriety to offer. Roger was brutal in his pronouncement that I was stupid and an embarrassment. Since many of the pretty girls in the school accepted his opinion on such matters as law, this was devastating to my social life. I did strike up a brief friendship with Ingrid, the one with the pouting lips and the staring eyes in the back row, third from left. She was actually a bright, sensitive girl who lived not far from our house and shared my love of reading and painting. She was my chief rival for the class prize in drawing. As our friendship grew, I naively alleged that she was my girlfriend, and this caused her great embarrassment in the Roger crowd. She had to forswear all knowledge of her friendship with me to regain her status. Ingrid became a teacher and married a police officer who was a great beater. He left her with a broken spirit and three children. She had a very hard life and two nervous breakdowns but was lucky to discover that her second son was very clever and a big success. He pays for all her medication and looks after her very well.

Roger had a sad life for he could never adjust to a world where his father was not God. He is now an administrator in a backwater civil service office and a mainstay of the rumshops in our area. He did get married – to a stenographer who told him one Saturday night that she was leaving next day to join her true love in the States, and walked out with their son and his self-respect.

The fierce looking boy with the squint is Natty, the class bully. Natty was enforcer for Bobby and other stars of the class. He used to chase me around the schoolyard to beat me up for the hell of it, and once banged my head on the tamarind tree in the middle of the churchyard next door. One rainy Friday afternoon, he and Bobby dragged Singh to the churchyard, pulled off his trousers and hung them up on the church bell tower. Mr Jarvis gave them twelve each when the matter was reported but Singh lost whatever status he had in our eyes and never managed to make any friends at all. He is the thin little guy with spectacles. We used to call him Pandit and I sometimes wished I had treated him better or tried to defend him, or even formed a club of the unpopular and the oppressed. Sadly, and to my shame, I joined in mocking Pandit during his many trials in the hope that the bullies would leave me alone if they had a more acceptable victim. Pandit never mentions these incidents when I take my mother to the hospital where he is a consultant. He treats me like an old buddy and ensures that we get the best attention reserved for old family friends. I try not to use the name Pandit since he is now a devout catholic, but he finds it funny so I suppose he has less bitter memories than I expected.

Natty? He became a labourer in the village council road gang but soon tired of that and went into the bush, and may still be there for all I know. No one in our area has heard of him for a long time.

The other Indian boy in the picture is Ray, the class disgrace. He was quite a character. He was a great skulker. He left home with his books and in his school clothes every day but knew an infinite variety of ways not to reach school. He could be at the Hollywood cinema for the one o'clock show, or he could be at the rifle range collecting shells, or he could be at the sea wall swimming, or he could be in the burial ground throwing dice with older strays, or he could be in Mr Green's yard feeding on downs and psidium and genips, or he could be in the gardens spying on naked lovers. He did turn up for a few days each week and managed to pass the school tests despite his varied agenda. He was also the best cricketer in the school and was the reason why we beat the government school in the next village in the challenge matches and the inter-school competitions every year. Ray could spoil a game with absurd bowling analyses like seven wickets for four runs and numbers like that. He could also bat. Mr Jarvis referred to him as "Slug-o-tom", of which name he was extremely proud. When he was batting, the ball could end up in somebody's yard or in the trench or through the church glass windows. The teachers all complained that he would come to no good and that his skulking and stray-boy companions would lead him to a horrible end, probably jail. Strangely, Ray is the classmate to whom I have become closest, for he is active in the PTA of the school my son attends. He is a generous donor to all fund-raising schemes. He is a strict father and there is no doubt that his children will all do well and go away to university, for they are not only bright but well behaved.

Ray runs a strict Hindu home with meticulous observation of domestic disciplple.

If anyone was expected to have a bright future, it was Colleen. She is the dark girl with full lips and the big ribbons. She was not part of any of the gangs. She did not partake in the dirty talk and she had no boyfriends. She was the pupil every teacher loves to have. Her essays were neatly written in a copybook hand with one-inch spaces between each word and all the recommended big words included. Her exercise books were neatly kept and her texts were well papered in colourful magazine pages. She was top in class every year for as long as I can remember, and all the teachers who knew anything about her said she would go far. She was always the teacher's pet and was forever being asked to sit at the teacher's desk to do special tasks. She was the child usually chosen to say "Tiger Tiger Burning Bright" or "It was Battered and Scarred the Old Violin" when the parson came to visit the school. She did Virgin Mary twice in the Christmas play during her days at school. Colleen is now in politics, a minor party functionary in a mining town far from here, and embarrassed me horribly when she came back for a wedding at which I was playing the role of the distinguished guest with a university degree. She explained in great detail how fat I was in our school days and described in pretty crude language where the extra weight located itself. She has become coarse and loud, though I suppose she must be an effective organiser for I gather she has been doing the same job for a very long time.

You learn a lot from old photographs.

Sonny Coming

S ONNY coming home at last. I will able to hold my head up in the village and catch swank on all the grudgeful jezebels we got around here. Sonny coming home and they will have to respect me now and give me honour what is my due. All them who wash they mouth pun me, who talk me name and call me words, who put they hand in front they mouth when I passing to skin they teeth, they will be put to silence. They will be put to shame. Especially she the Marie Jones who daughter make she eyes pass my Sonny and tell the boy she don't associate with riffraff and other hurtful things when he ask she to go to dance with he. Sonny never say a word to me, he is not that kind of boy, but she the Marie had was to meet me in the market and give me a good busing that how my son black and ugly and she daughter have she good colour and don't need to entangle with people like me. That child think she is it because she is the one who used to get pick for the May Queen and act as Princess Margaret in the school play. I shame so till, because is right there in public the woman embarrass me. And where the Ingrid Jones now is what I say, where she deh? My Sonny is coming back to make me proud before the whole world and she the Ingrid can't catch sheself since she end up in purgatory with the white man from she office. I want to see Marie face when my Sonny come home.

I is not a spiteful woman and I don't bear a grudge but when I hold my thanksgiving dinner for my Sonny, they have some people who I mad to invite for all the things they do me but is better they come so I can see they face when my doctor son stand up and tell them how much his mother do for him. Like parson. That man is a real hypocrite, you hear. When my Sonny ask that man for a recommendation to get he first job, the amount of styles he make like he is a fashion book. And he was one of the first to advise he against going to America and say how American doctors not recognise in the colony and he should accept the Lord will and stay teacher right here in BG. Is the truth I telling you. If I lie, let the maker strike me down. He wanted to hold my boy back. He didn't want to see no little black boy get up. But my Sonny is coming back as a doctor, chile, he is Doctor Wilfred Bentley, and the same reverend will have to swallow he white saliva and give God thanks for what my Sonny has done.

How long Sonny been away? Is nearly ten years, mi'dear. Ten long years, and how I punish in them times. Not one of my family lift a finger to help me in that time. Girl I not shame to tell you I see some hard times in them years before Sonny could afford to send me a lil something to keep me going. I had to start back taking in washing, walking every night to deliver the clothes and fighting that tub every morning. And with this hand giving me the works, it was a punishment. Well now is time to take my ease and laloff. Is this Berbice chair shall be my portion from now on.

Of course I will invite Teach, that wretch. He and that big-foot wife who trying to hide her infirmities behind all kind of long dress and trousers. I never tell you the story? When my Sonny take scholarship, he was the best in the class and Teacher Willie would beat that boy just so to discourage him and bring up he own son. He give that child a time, you hear. Yet for all of that, Sonny cut they tail in the exam but you know how this country stay, Teach get together with he friends in the department and he son get in and my Sonny had to catch hell. I hear Teacher Willie say that he give Sonny he start in life! Start in life? I only hope that he don't take in sick and Sonny is the doctor who have to save he life cause is dead he dead.

Sonny coming back, chile, Sonny coming back.

Every time I think of the morning he left on that boat to go away, I feel like crying all over again. Was hard, Nennen, was hard. Was just a few people on the wharf. All them other people had big family to see them off and is only me and you and his friends from the government school who was there for him. I know I did behave bad but they had a lil big-eye one who say she was his sweetheart and start up one bawling and I couldn't make she show me up in front of John Public so I had to put down a bawling too. Sonny get shame-face and climb on the boat more quick, but he was always like that. What happen to big-eye whoshenim? She uses to come here wid she kang-ga-langs and bring me card and gift and thing. But from how she used to talk, I not too sure if Sonny even used to write she. Then she get scarce and I thought she done married off only to find that she lef right deh. Since she hear Sonny coming back, she start coming here again. But a telling you one thing, with the size she put on I don know if Sonny gon able with she but I not getting into the young gentleman business. I know you did tell me some story about she and the Inspector but the woman is a respectable teacher girl and I can't afford to give my mouth liberty. I will give Sonny the facts and he is his own big man.

That teacher job was a blessing. Even though was only a small piece he used to get, the boy would bring it home straight and it was monthly money, girl, monthly money. When I think of all the years I spend in my life paying church dues and baking patties for their damn bible class, and making sugar cake and bread for harvest, it hurt my heart to know that he had to look for work in a government school in the country. Is train every day he had to take, but he hold on and take his exams one by one and is so he apply to the States.

How he get the passage? Girl, I not really sure. He had a bank book but he didn't have much to put, teachers not so well paid. I can tell you one thing, is not his father who help him. That man is not going to put his foot in this yard as God is my witness. He is the one badman I not inviting to enjoy my special day. The one time me and my son come wrong is when I hear that Mister man used to present his wutless self at my son school to beg for a freck. Sonny have too much good mind. I tell he how his father never do anything for him and how he never pay a cent for his education and how the man rather take jail than pay child support. All the boy say to that was, "But is still my father." Children could be so ungrateful sometimes. But is one thing I saying is that he not coming here to see my son and he will have to duck and hide by the boy doctor shop if he want anything from he. Not in here!

My Sonny coming back, he coming home!

What we gone eat? Well I think he gone want some cook-up and some dry food. That is what he does always say when he write and I have set ginger beer even though is not Christmas. Is a strange thing, he also say that how he does wake up in the middle of the night longing for ochro and strimps, you believe that? America must be really have bad food.

Anyhow he coming home to his mother kitchen and my sweet hand. No, is Mr Rogers making the arrangements. He done arrange for the pass to go on the wharf and book a taxi from Prem. Don't worry to cut up yuh eye. Ah know you don't like Mr Rogers but is none of your business and I have no complaints. The man has his responsibilities and I has to have discretion.

Stop minding my business and leh we start planning for Mr Sonny.

Sugrim, Patrick and Me

S UGRIM, Patrick and I were best friends. Sugrim was very poor, had horrible sores covering his legs, very few schoolbooks and wrote on a slate with only one side of its wooden frame remaining. Teacher Constance referred to it as a chopper. Patrick, however, was the son of a pan-boiler at the estate and was therefore treated with great deference by the teachers. He was often allowed to leave school mid-morning to carry his father's breakfast to the factory. No one seemed to think this was strange. I was the only son of Teacher Waveney so I was an aristocrat among my classmates. Patrick was a "dougla". I did not know at the time what that meant but I knew it was something exotic and possibly shameful, and it was often the cause of comment by my mother and other teachers, who clearly thought that being a dougla was a terrible thing to happen to a young child.

We did many things together, the three of us. Patrick and Sugrim and I were avid cricketers and since I always owned a tennis or rubber ball of some kind, I was always made captain for inter-class matches. I was always glad to have them both on my team for they played cricket extremely well. This was not always possible during "first pick" games, where the captains had to pick a man in turn, since either Patrick or Sugrim were often captains in their own right. During the week, we had ordinary "first and second" at recreation and after school. The headteacher would take us through our singsong representation of the various prayers. We would say the doxology and shout, "Now and forever more, Amen, FIRST! FIRST! SECOND! SECOND!" This was your position in the afternoon batting order. First shout, first bat. I was cunning, I started shouting, "THIRD! THIRD!" so that all unsuccessful claimants to the top positions came behind me in the queue. On Fridays, we played "get-the-ball-bowl-out-the-man-bat". This was exactly what it said and produced enthusiastic if dangerous fielding since the fieldsman was credited with the batsman's dismissal if a catch was involved. Big bullies like me were liable to knock small fry from their legitimate catches to get a chance to bat again. Patrick, however, had a genius for being where a catch was sure to go without having to resort to rugby tactics.

We also sat together in class. Sugrim was good at sums and mental. I was good at transcription and composition. I was also good at leading the tables chant in the afternoon session. "One and one are two," I would screech. The class would chant the same words and the same tune: "ONE AND ONE ARE TWO!"

Patrick was a dunce who wrote very badly and could not spell at all. But he was confident and forward and always had good excuses for his deficiencies. When I pointed out to him that there was a story about cricket in the reading book, he was forever in my debt and read it so often that he could recite the extract from "Tom Brown's Schooldays" by heart. This feat served him in good stead when the school's inspectors came. These were grim, impressive-looking men with large briefcases and bald heads. The teachers lived in fear for the entire week and the lady teachers called us "dearheart" and "baby" and the men teachers hid their tamarind whips. The inspectors called on our class to give a demonstration of our reading skills and Patrick was expected to bring down the class average. Patrick surprised Teacher Constance with his brilliant and confident reading, however, and rattled off the story word perfect. Only Sugrim and I knew that Patrick could not read anything else in the West Indian Reader. Patrick was the darling of Miss for days afterwards and was entrusted with key errands such as returning the class register to the headmaster's table and taking notes to Mr Stone at Standard IV.

Sugrim brought his breakfast in a saucepan, wrapped in a coloured cloth with a battered spoon stuck in the topknot. It was always rice and curry something. Not much something I might add and, in tough times, not readily recognised as curry anything. Patrick's breakfast was packed in a carrier, three enamel pans with a common handle. Each pan contained a separate part of the breakfast. The rice might come in one, the stew in another, the ground provisions in another. Patrick was from a good family. I had to eat my breakfast from a thermos flask that kept everything hot from morning. I had such varied meals as metem, cook-up, chow mein and channa. My mother also packed a bag with knife, fork, spoon, towel and other embarrassments. It took several minutes to unpack her handiwork but I did not complain, or relay the contempt of my companions, for I knew that many of the senior teachers frowned upon her allowing me to eat with the riffraff in the first place. The other women had regarded this as part of her generally lax and liberal attitudes to serious matters. I lived with the dread that I might be forced to eat with her and all those old women, and use the knife and fork. Sometimes Sugrim's saucepan was suspiciously light and the curry on the rice would be just a smear but he never complained and, much to my mother's worry, readily traded with me for part of my food.

In marble season, we formed a consortium to control the button market. All games were played for buttons. Rollbounce, gam, three-hole, all had to be tallied and paid for with buttons. I was the supplier of buttons with which to finance losers who had exhausted their supply, had raided their trousers' crotches and their shirts. When all else had failed, they came to me for supplies, which I had uplifted from my granny's market stall. Since Sugrim and Patrick were the champions at marbles, it was only natural that we should collaborate, and having sold buttons at four a cent, I shared my loot with them and we grew wealthy in this trade. Unfortunately, marble season was only temporary and bucktop became the rage. To make a top, you obtained a large awara seed and, having placed two holes at the two tips and one at the side, you removed the kernel inside and put a pole through the middle. A short stick spins the top with a hole at one end and a length of string. I achieved notoriety by using my toothbrush handle to start my top. My mother found out about this experiment and it cost me several blows with the broom. Sugrim was the master of the top. He had a craftsman's touch and his tops were bigger and neater than everyone else's. They sang and spun for ages. Mine were puny efforts by comparison.

Kite season lasted a long time. It started as soon as your toys from Christmas fell apart. That meant that your colt .45 and your holster had fallen apart or that your supply of caps had run out. That was Patrick and I: Sugrim never had any toys. We started small with pointer sticks stuck through pages torn from books. Then we graduated to pointer frames pasted with flimsy "kite paper" and stuck to the frame with glamma cherry berries. I had all the materials for kite making, including number 0 crochet thread raided from Mum and Granny. I also got a modest stock of kite paper free from Granny's stall. I could not make kites to match the beauty of those by Sugrim and Patrick. Their kites lasted longer, sailed higher and sang more impressively than my own creations. Fortunately, I was a master at kite fighting, which involved putting a safety razor or other nasty instrument in the tail of your kite and cutting the string of other people's. Unfortunately we did not see each other on Easter Monday since that was in the holidays and I had to go to Georgetown to fly kites with my stuck-up cousins from the city. I always returned to school with an exaggerated story of the size of my kite and the colours it displayed, and the feebleness of the kite fliers in Georgetown.

We were separated by promotion to Standard V and the selection of people for the scholarship class. Scholarship class sat on the raised area called the stage at the western end of the schoolroom. It was presided over by the head himself and they sat under his wing along with the pupil teachers studying for "appointment" exams. The class on stage was for those in whom high hopes were placed and on whom the head could lavish his attentions. He was, as was often the case in those days, a great beater. Some days he would fly into a rage and beat all the scholarship class on some pretext. Often he was very bizarre, as at the time when he flogged all girls in the school who had multicoloured ribbons in their hair. Those who went to the scholarship class were the envy and pity of the rest of the school for they were flogged often and in full view. For the pupil teachers, the stage was doubly embarrassing since they were teachers themselves with flogging privileges.

I assumed that the brightest students with good passing papers and high places in the tests would be selected. Strangely, however, Sugrim, a naturally bright boy, was not selected and the Mangra girl, whose father owned a drug store, was. I got selected since my mother was a teacher, though I was only average. Patrick the dunce was also chosen. Patrick never enjoyed school, books or scholarship class. His exercise books were usually folded in his back pocket. He was beaten as often as his father's status at the estate would allow. He never developed an interest in books or the exam, and after the scholarship exam he drifted into young adult life and became a drunkard and womaniser. Inexplicably, many years later, he committed suicide.

I endured the scholarship class and I probably owe it to my mother that I was not beaten as often as I deserved. I also suspect that once the head realised that I had no chance of getting a pass, he lost interest in me as a potential source of glory. My grandparents paid for me to go to a little high school in town and I slipped into the police force for want of anything better to do. Sugrim left school shortly after I was put in the special class. I never knew what had become of him and often wondered where he was.

Many years later, I was posted to the coast as officer-in-charge and a team of farmers asked to see me concerning an outbreak of cattle rustling. They came into the office dressed in their best white shirts, brown pants, and felt hats clutched in their hands. Some had on yachting shoes and one even had shoes on, brown and unlaced. The leader of the delegation kept smiling at me in a strange way and it took some time before I recognised him. It was Sugrim, now a respectable farmer and community leader. I blurted out my recognition and my pleasure at seeing my old buddy. He remained deferential and constrained by the combination of my uniform, my rank and by his efforts to speak proper English.

We promised to keep in touch but I guess we never will.

We were best friends, Sugrim, Patrick and I.

The Big Fight

Ours is a quiet town. Anthony Trollope visited us on his travels as a young man and thought that he felt as if Rip Van Winkle lived here and no one remembered to wake him up. That is unfair. We are a quiet town but I do not believe we are asleep. We have our moments and we have our history. The Berbice river washes past our town and by the time she gets to us she has gone by the old capital where the slaves had rebelled two hundred years ago, slaughtered the planters and declared themselves free. The river has to go by all the old Dutch plantations with the histories of treachery, death, betrayal and hidden treasure. All good ghost stories begin with a dead Dutch planter and an old silk-cotton tree, with perhaps a slave mistress or two thrown in for good measure. The river sees all of that before it reaches our town.

Many of our people have escaped our town for the big city; I suppose they were seduced by the story that our town was so sleepy and the city is wide awake. So they cross the river and catch the train for the city, never to return.

I love this town because life is so simple and predictable. You know who is who and what is what. On Saturday mornings you go to market. On Saturday afternoons you buy parched peanuts for the children and black pudding and souse for the wife. Then you go for a drink with the boys. On Sundays you go to church. Then you have soup for breakfast. Soup made with ochro or peas and laden with ground provisions and accompanied by a plate of foo-foo, pounded by the wife with her own mortar stick. And breakfast is at midday, not morning. In the morning you have tea. After breakfast you have a nap then get dressed again and go to the promenade or the gardens. You give deference to the important people and you know who they are. The old respectable families who have no whiff of scandal in their record and can be relied upon to maintain culture in the town. Our street is quiet like the rest of our town. We have no need to lock our doors. Who would even dream of stealing from anyone else? We are so quiet here that one midnight when the neighbours saw the lights on in our house, all the women dressed and came over because they knew someone had to be sick.

But there was one brief moment of infamy when our little street became known to the entire colony, and we became notorious in the Court Proceedings pages of the city dailies. I suppose it started when Dutchie came to live in the old cottage at the end of the street. She was a tall and striking brown woman who just appeared suddenly one morning walking behind a donkey cart with some household furniture and assorted bags and parcels. She was called Dutchie for she had come from Dutch Guiana, the colony east of us. No one knew who she was, where she came from or why she had come to this town and this sleepy street. She introduced herself to no one and made no friends. She made no attempt to become part of the street life, and though she had no visible means of support she went to market regularly and was always well dressed as she paraded past, head held high. We did not know her real name. She was just Dutchie. When some more adventurous people made attempts to engage her in conversation, she answered to the name Dutchie with polite recognition and made no attempt to make us any the wiser.

New versions of her history circulated by spit press every few weeks, each one more lurid and exciting than the one before. Some included spectacular tales of murder, betrayal, the Dutch police and one particularly gruesome story involving a butcher's knife and a ship's captain. This was delivered to me by the wife who, like all the women in the street, was offended that such a handsome and mysterious woman could appear on her doorstep with no reliable history for her to digest.

This was so unlike Finey, the other exotic woman in our street. Finey was an extremely pretty young Indian girl from the Courantyne who lived with Samson, the ruler of a popular rumshop on Pitt Street. She was the product of a fine devout home, the youngest daughter of a successful rice farmer. For some reason, when the time had come for her to be safely married into a respectable family of her mother's choosing, she had fled to town and found herself in a bawdy house in Pitt Street, where she made a precarious living before being taken up by Samson as his mistress. She had, of course, long since been renounced by her relatives and had become an established part of the street network.

My wife and her cronies pretended to be shocked by the presence in our street of someone who had done unspeakable things in Pitt Street. But since Finey was a pretty and cheerful girl, and since her tragic differences with her family made her an intriguing topic for conversation, she was always well treated by the other women in the street. Finey and Samson had no children and she therefore had little to do during the day apart from cook for Samson and wash his clothes, so she spent a lot of time "looking out". This idleness did not cause her to gain weight, for at the time of the arrival of Dutchie she was still a thin little woman, well described by her name.

I know that I claimed that we are a quiet street but we do have our moments. Every so often, when Samson came home in the wee hours after closing his rumshop, he and Finey would have some terrible rows. Usually, it was about Finey's suspicion that he was extending his goodness to other women. Since she no longer frequented Pitt Street, I am at a loss to know how she received her facts about Samson, but she would let him have it. For such a little woman, who was so well brought up, Finey had a wonderful capacity for quarrelling. It came out in streams, invective upon invective, detail upon detail, and she had a range of cuss words which impressed even Doghouse, my drinking pal and a sailor with wide experience in these matters. Sometimes, Samson simply ignored her and went to sleep. This was not too difficult for him; Samson was a taciturn man. Even in his bar he said very little and, though his rumshop was a lively and noisy spot, he contributed very little to this atmosphere and conducted all business and served his guests in a permanent state of irritability and annoyance. Some mornings, however, he would decide that he had had enough and issue a few resounding slaps. He even took off his belt on one occasion and we heard the thwack of leather on delicate skin, then sobs, and then silence. That was rare though. Usually, when Finey was jealous and annoyed, she had her say and Samson went to sleep.

One Saturday morning, very early and before all reasonable people were awake, Finey and Samson got into an extra serious set to. The mistress woke me up to join her in listening to the row, and though at first I was upset and steupsed, I realised why she wanted me among the audience. It appears that somehow Finey had procured information to the effect that Dutchie was an old lover of her gentleman, and that he had arranged to assist her flight from the Dutch police and was now assisting her by generous gifts from the rumshop profits. Samson actually said a few words in his defence, but Finey's outrage was louder and more passionate than usual. Eventually, Samson left his house, presumably to seek comfort from some of his stock.

At dayclean, Dutchie presented herself at the bridge to Finey's yard and challenged Finey in loud and heavily accented English to come out and face her. To my surprise, Finey did emerge and repeated her allegations, specifying sums of money and mysterious dirty habits. Dutchie was no match for Finey in cursing, since she was not at home in English and since she sometimes paused for breath. I doubt she truly understood all the curses she received but Finey had a knack for putting on an expression of pure obscenity when describing the evils Dutchie used to take away her man and his money. The wife kept saying, "Is a shame, is a shame. We have children in this house." She then pulled up a chair and put her right eye to a hole in the wall so she would not miss any of the action. Eventually, Dutchie could take it no longer and began to give Finey a good beating. She was big and strong and seemed very experienced. Finey was young and quick and had long nails and sharp teeth, but she could not resist the power of the strapping red woman, and you know how red women are when they get angry. It seemed as if Finey was being badly hurt under the rain of blows, and many of the more public-spirited citizens were already forming a circle and making peace-keeping efforts. I wanted to go out and join them but Maggie kept pulling me back inside and grumbling incoherently about low-class mess.

Finey seemed to have no defence, for Dutchie had locked her off with the left and kept pummelling her with the right, oblivious of the feeble scratches and kicks from Finey. The fight migrated from the gate to the grass corner, thence to the drain and the plimpla bush, and thence to some soft mud and bisi-bisi. It was then that Finey used her head and took the vital steps that saved her from a serious mauling from the Dutch Amazon. Finey reached for the front of Dutchie's dress and tore it apart. Dutchie's large pale-brown breasts were exposed to the early morning light, and with so many men among the potential referees she had to leave off beating Finey to protect her modesty, vainly trying to piece together her clothes and cover her chest at the same time. Finey dashed to safety and, seeing a loose wallaba stave on the fence, she pulled if off and turned to give Dutchie a blow. Dutchie was in confusion. Should she protect her modesty or her head? In the end, she failed to do either. A nasty gash spouted blood from Dutchie's forehead and Finey lost all her fire. She dropped the stave and, in shock at what she had done, sat down in the middle of the road, sobbing and mumbling to herself.

Obviously, I had to go over and render first aid to Dutchie and help Miss Tinney staunch the blood and cover her with a sheet prior to taking her on my bicycle to the hospital. The wife did not forgive me for weeks for my gallant intervention. But she is so confusing. Rather than complaining about my nearness to the unveiled Dutchie, she complained for days about the risk of having to give a statement to the police or, even worse, of having to testify in court in a "niggeryard story". Of course, Finey was charged with "wounding with intent" and Dutchie was charged with disturbing the peace and disorderly conduct. The papers had fun. The "Rumshop Romeo" and "Women at War" are the headlines I remember best.

Samson refused to have anything to do with either woman and flatly refused to give a statement when asked by the police. When he answered a summons to attend court, he cut a surly figure and upset both the magistrate and the lawyer defending Finey. The magistrate had many things to say in his judgement about evil men and loose women. Samson remained unmoved by the sentencing of his women and returned to his rumshop to serve the drinks as reluctantly as ever.

He has recently installed a plump little Amerindian girl in his cottage.

I know I said our town is really quiet, but every now and then these things do happen.

The Dance

MY father and Brother Singh finally made up their minds. They were
going to hold a picnic on August Monday to raise money for their
burial society. August Monday was a holiday for something or other, I
forget the details now, and was a popular spot in the calendar for outings,
dances, weddings and other forms of festivity. You must understand that
this decision by these two gentlemen was a source of shock to all who
knew them. They were not planning to hold a family gathering on the sea
wall or in the botanical gardens, or even on the back-dam which protected
our village from the floodwaters, which always threatened to flood our
village on the coast of Guyana, east of Georgetown. "Picnic" in Guyana is
a euphemism for a public dance held in the daytime. My dad and his
friend were planning to hold a dance with food, music and, wonder of
wonders, dancing.

That my father, the assistant pastor of the Pentecostal Church of
Holiness (with headquarters in Tulsa, Oklahoma), and his friend, the
presiding elder of the Assembly of Spiritual Brethren, should be planning
to hold a dance was a surprise which undermined the foundations of all
the certainties that had hitherto confined my young life. You see, my
father was renowned for his imprecations and condemnation of all forms
of worldliness, pleasure seeking, and all things of the flesh. Brother Singh
was wont to issue his strictures to the young people in his chapel with a
mild manner and his high-pitched nasal recitation of all the eternal
penalties of youthful lusts, particularly calypso singing and that evil of
evils, jazz. My Dad on the other hand was a blood and thunder destroyer
of all partakers of the sins of the flesh. He believed in the liberal use of fiery
texts on hell and was particularly fond of passages where the Philistines
and Amalekites were slain, both man and beast. Many nights I walked
home from Sunday night gospel meetings, with his loud, booming bass
voice ringing in my ears, and expecting as I walked along the east coast
train tracks to meet one of the fearful bearded holy men who slew the
prophets of Baal and destroyed the enemies of the chosen people from
Geba to Geza. Many Sundays, my father's wrath against sinners would
reach its climax with a condemnation of those who destroyed their souls
by dancing. He called it "the danceall" and managed to inject so much
scorn and condemnation into his pronunciation of that word that I
imagined that people who went into such places came out covered with

some invisible coating of sinful slime as they danced their way to the bottomless pit. This was the man who wanted to hold a picnic to raise money.

Mum did not think too much of my Dad's preaching. She had been brought up as an Anglican and was conditioned to the well-ordered and polite rituals of the English-born priest at St James the Greater on the main public road. She always felt that by marrying a preacher in a "claphand", "duck-o-pond" church, she had taken a step down the village social ladder. Being a dutiful wife and, truth be told, having a pliable and harmless husband, she loyally attended the Pentecostal Church of Holiness Chapel with my father, but she let him have the full benefit of her disgust when we got back home. As soon as the family reached home from church, my mother would light into dad. "But Ben, why you have to preach for such a long time? Catholic finished, Anglican finished, even Brethren finished and passing our church on the way home. Yet you carry on and on and on. Just how you long so your story long." My father was well over six feet tall.

The two elders of the faith met at our house to plan their grand picnic. They sat mumbling to each other on a wooden bench on our little porch. Each house had one of those in the old days, what we called the platform. My mother sent us to play under the house, the "bottom-house", which everyone had since all our homes were built on stilts to keep us dry in the rainy season or in case the sea wall should break down. After reviewing the general laxity of morals in the village, and regretting the lewd, sinful, profane, devil's music with which the ZFY radio station was corrupting the minds of sinners everywhere, they got down to the business of planning their grand event in aid of the Wilberforce Village Burial and Friendly Society, the basis of my father's venture as an impresario.

The burial society was the main, indeed the only, financial institution in the village. Members put in small contributions on a weekly basis (at that time I believe it was a shilling) and were guaranteed most of the expenses of a funeral when they died. Nothing worried our people more than the thought that they would die and not have the resources to afford to ask a cabinet-maker to give a good coffin, or to afford a good "send-off". Your family could endure years of shame if your coffin was cheap or your funeral shabby. The only thing more satisfying to your relatives than the size of the crowd would be to hear the approving comments of important people at your funeral remarking on the beauty and dignity of your coffin. The burial society was therefore important as a guard against embarrassment. Most of us in Wilberforce village were poor.

The society also gave small loans in times of trouble. Just before Christmas, provided there was no serious outbreak of death or bad debts, the society gave a bonus to its members, which was put to good use on buying toys for children or rum for fathers, depending on the priorities of the household. Anyway, it appeared that there were either more deaths than forecast or too many loans, because evidently Dad, the society chairman, and Brother Singh, its treasurer, foresaw a decline in the level of bonuses payable that coming Christmas, a disaster and embarrassment which neither man could afford. Indeed, it appeared possible that no bonus might be paid at all, calling into question the stewardship of the two saints. This would have marked the end of their joint reign as the heads of the society. There were other village notables willing and able to stand for high office, including the postmaster as well as the senior assistant teacher at the Anglican school, a noted critic of sanctimonious do-gooders such as my father.

The two good men had much difficulty arranging their picnic, since neither of them had any experience in such activities, which needed the collaboration of notorious sinners and worldly types. Eventually, with the aid of advice from my disgraced uncle, Mum's brother, and unsolicited comments from my mother, the event was arranged. Pereira was booked to provide rum, ice and "two-glass quenchers", Boy-boy was engaged to re-arrange the school furniture in a manner suitable for dancing, and Scotty was engaged to write and display a large, crude notice near the train station, announcing:

A GRAND AUGUST MONDAY PICNIC,
ST JAMES ANGLICAN SCHOOL HALL.
ADMISSION TWO SHILLINGS.
MUSIC BY THE POPULAR SCRUBBING BOARD ORCHESTRA.

My father had somehow managed – during a trip to town – to engage the magical and famous band. How he had found out where to make the arrangements, and how he managed to get them for this, the most popular date for daytime partying, is a mystery which he took with him to his grave.

There was no question, of course, that any of his children or his wife would be allowed to attend this infamous affair. While he was quite content to collect money from sinners for a good cause, he was not going to endanger the souls of his beloved children if he could help it. On August Monday, my father ventured forth dressed in a flowered shirt which he hoped was suitable for the occasion.

I managed to see the arrival of the Scrubbing Boards by a variety of stratagems that conned my mother into sending me on an errand in the vicinity of the Anglican school. The band came by train and walked to the school while their instruments were fetched on a donkey cart hired from Drunken-Tommy. The elders spared no pains. The bandsmen appeared to be jolly and hearty fellows, aware of the eyes on them and anxious to impress the locals. There was much back-slapping and loud laughter and jive talk. I decided there and then that a band musician was the most wonderful life there was on earth, and the wondrous instruments, saxophones, trombones and drums, made me forget how wicked they were supposed to be. I returned home and felt guilty when my mother asked me, with her twinkle in the eye, why it had taken me so long to do one small errand.

Later that day, my mother committed a profound act of sedition. She took me and Baby Sis to visit Sister Singh, which allowed her to walk past the sinful goings-on in the Anglican School. Also, I should point out that the village had never forgiven the Johnson girl for marrying a "coolie", as Bro. Singh was called behind his back. This despite the fact that Brother Singh had long since renounced his Hindu upbringing and his high caste for Christianity, and despite the fact that his job at the sugar estate gave him a regular monthly salary, and entitled him to work at a desk in a suit and a tie. There were even sinister rumours that Sister Singh had learned to cook roti and curry. Dad had made dark threats over the consequences if Mum ever tried to cook such heathenish food in his house. I had my own seditious motives as I walked alongside my mother to the Singh's house, for I was deeply fascinated with their daughter, a curly-haired beauty called Doro, and I sometimes suspected that when my father condemned the lusts of the flesh consuming the youth, he had sneaked into the hidden recesses of my young imaginings.

Our afternoon walk enabled us to witness the total humiliation of my father and his friend. For despite the sweetness of the band and Pereira's two-glass quenchers, the sinners resolutely refused to pay to enter the burial society picnic. As we passed, the band was playing the hit song "Cherry Pink And Apple Blossoms White", and as we moved further on they broke into a swing version of "Daddy Let Me Stay Out Late". Just two couples were dancing in a desultory manner in the school building, and the large crowd on the public road was already hurling taunts at the two men sitting pompously at the door waiting to collect their money. Mum is a lady and she passed the picnic with her head in the air, her parasol swinging with elegance.

But she did not spare him when eventually, not being a loiterer, Dad had to come home. "Other people giving dance, you not going. You only condemning the dance people in the church. Now you giving dance and you expect other people to come."

Then she gave one of her long suck-teeths. It rang through the house that Monday night as my father dragged his tired and defeated self into bed. I believe the scorn of his wife was worse than the public humiliation he received. Doro agrees with me.

The Visitation

I T was definite. The news was confirmed. THEY were coming. This was the biggest event in the village and our house was the very centre of all the excitement. No one was able to talk about anything else for days. THEY were coming and THEY would be there together. The two greatest men in the colony, the Doctor and the Kabaka, were to attend a special meeting of the Brotherhood and Sisterhood Movement. The Movement was a gathering of all church-going and respectable types in the village, responsible for good works and the network of clubs and groups arranged to bring about the "uplift" of people in our area. Generally, their activity seemed to me to consist of anniversaries and concerts in each other's churches and school halls, and made a good excuse to have an annual dance at which the village elite could let their hair down and have a ball in public, as opposed to having their fun in secret as was usually the case. Since this movement was, however, a gathering of the important, it was fitting THEY should be invited to visit.

The Doctor was of course a celebrity in his own right. Had he not returned with a white wife and proceeded to shake up the political forces of society? Had he not challenged the Governor and the white people with his outlandish views? Had he not taught us new words such as "democracy", "the people", "revolutionary", "exploitation" and "change"? Besides, many people in the village had gone to his surgery and had told us of his charm and, more importantly, his reasonable fees.

But the Kabaka. He was truly our boy. He was from right here in our group, had gone to school right here in the very schoolroom in which the Movement was holding its meeting. He had gone on to great things at the college and his name was mentioned to young victims like myself in the same breath with others whose deeds could only be described by use of all their given names. (I have since been trying to figure out the subtleties which determine that my uncle Gavin is called Brown but his childhood neighbour was called Edgar Mortimer Duke. Always.) The Kabaka was like that. He had gone to the big college and scored a Guiana. The Guiana. The coveted scholarship which brought prestige and glory to its holders and all their connections, and established the holder amongst the deities of Creole society; and HE was coming.

The coming was important to our household. Mum had to prepare the snacks. That was understood. No one asked her. It was assumed that she would be in charge and anyone wanting to assist could join her on the great day. I was dragged into the occasion, for it had recently been discovered that I had taught myself to play the harmonium by ear, and on festive occasions held at what to Mr Jones, the official player, were inconvenient times, such as Sunday afternoons, I was deputed to play "God Save The Queen", the "Doxology", and to accompany any soloists who had not brought an accompanist. This was not as difficult as it might seem since the range of solos was quite confined and "Cherry Ripe", "Where the Bee Sucks" and "Where'er You Walk" covered a large part of my needs. Since THEY were coming, Mr Jones was bound to turn up, but I was forced to be there as insurance. Baby Sis had to go because not to send her with me might cause me to have fun with no one to report back to HQ.

Strangely, however, Dad – who should have been the most excited – was most miserable concerning the whole exercise. He, being the village pot salt, would have to be the chairman on the great day. Further, it was rumoured that, with the British planning to hold elections by universal adult suffrage in the near future, the Movement was choosing candidates for the various districts, and Dad was likely to become the representative for this district and sit in the Legco. As the day drew near, I heard the adults in the house engaged in intense conversation and once, when Uncle Gavin was there, Dad gave a long and bitter denunciation of the Movement, warning that they were all communists and atheists and would lead the country into perdition and wickedness. He even prophesied that the two heroes would destroy the colony if they ever got hold of it from the British. Gavin and Mum got extremely angry at that point, accusing Dad of a love for kowtowing to white people and things like that, but Dad was implacable in his prophecies.

It never ceased to amaze me that, feeling the way he did, my father spent so much time preparing for the great visitation. He wore his best going-to-wedding suit and gave Mum a hard time in unwanted guidance over the preparation of the refreshments and their movement to the school hall. In those days THEY generated tremendous emotional energy wherever they went. The school was decorated with flowers and an array of potted plants. One of the schoolteachers had written a great welcome sign across the stage, and Mrs Murray's best tablecloth disguised our dining table that was set up for the personalities on stage. Such dignitaries as the Anglican priest and the headmasters were early to their places on the stage, and as the hall filled up the buzz of anticipation grew and the emotional temperature went up as if by some magic hand.

From my position at the ancient harmonium I heard the subdued gasp, the slamming of car doors and the shuffle of shoes which signalled their arrival, and the two heroes came in led by my father and other village notables suffering in the Sunday afternoon heat in their best dark serge suits. The Doctor and the Kabaka came in, both smiling and greeting friends and acquaintances in the crowd. The Kabaka sealed the day's excitement by remembering the name of an old classmate from his days in the village school. The Doctor was a handsome man, stunning in a white suit topped with his trademark spotted bow tie, so beloved of cartoonists in the dailies. The Kabaka was taller and dressed in a darker suit. They both had the gift of being able to attract your attention and keep you concentrated on them without seeming to do anything special.

Despite his Jeremiah performance at home, my Dad was surprisingly enthusiastic and efficient in getting the meeting going. After prayers by the priest, he introduced the two heroes as sons of the soil and asked them to take over. The Doctor spoke first in his strident and riveting style. He was probably uncomfortable in the company but if he was, he did not show it. His ideas about the evils of colonialism were new in those days and he illustrated his brief talk with a string of quotations from writers and politicians even the schoolteachers in our midst did not know. He was given generous applause at the end of his talk. We were ready to expel every white man from the colony and join the world. Then the Kabaka spoke. His voice was different and his style was different. The Doctor left us with more facts than I could remember. The Kabaka created an environment and it seemed then that their styles complemented each other, though I was never to hear them in tandem in that way again. The Kabaka was like easy-listening. Whenever I listen to a jazz set and the band move into a seductive arrangement with a clarinet or alto sax playing subtle riffs with the drum subdued, I remember the little speech that night. Strange it is however, though I was still too young to appreciate the quality of the minds at work in the Doctor and the Kabaka, I still knew that I was in the presence of greatness. I cannot remember anything that the Kabaka said apart from the joke he made at the very beginning of his speech. He pointed out that when he left the colony to study there were those who thought, because of his association with the church, that he was studying for the priesthood. But he remarked that there were limits to his hypocrisy. A lot of what the Doctor said then would probably annoy me today but then it all felt so good.

They all felt good, the people in that meeting. How they worshipped their idols and pledged their loyalty to the struggle for dignity and independence. How they surrounded them and pushed to get attention. One of my strange memories is of the Irish Methodist pastor, who was so fawning in his desire to be noticed and recognised that all my assumptions about the relationship between black and white became permanently confused.

My dad never made the Legco. When called upon a few weeks later to pledge his loyalty, he remained resolute in his opposition to what he called godless communism, and so annoyed the Kabaka that he was cut from the political list and faded into obscurity when THEY came to their Kingdom.

Guyanese Glossary

awara	a forest-palm bearing edible red fruit
back-dam	an earth dam at the rear of all coastal villages and estates in Guyana; it protects against flood, holds a freshwater reservoir and is a recreational area
battle pan, batel	a round metal strainer used in the process of separating gold-bearing gravel from soil
Berbice chair	a chair for reclining
BG	the colony British Guiana, now Guyana
bisi-bisi, bizzi-bizzi	a sedge or sturdy grass-like reed
boviander	a person with one Amerindian parent, the other black or European
choka	a puree fried in oil
corial	an Amerindian river canoe
danceman	a performer at Hindu celebrations
down	a small, apple-shaped plum
duck-o-pond	term applied to churches that practise immersion baptism
flouncer	a traditional character dancer in a masquerade band
foffie-eye, fofi-eye	an eye with a discoloured, whitish eyeball
foo-foo, fufu	pounded boiled plantain, yam or cassava, served with soup
freck	a small amount of money given in charity
gaff	patter, spiel, a glib persuasive line of talk
genip, guinep	also chenep, chennette, kenip, mapo, skinip, tjennet; a big deciduous tree with edible fruit
glamma, clammy-cherry	a small round fruit with a sweet sticky pulp
high-wine	a colourless liquor, a strong dilute form of the first product in the distillation of rum
houri, hoori	a small but nourishing river fish
Imbaimadai	a mining village in the Pakaraimas, famous in pork-knocker lore
Kabaka	the traditional paramount chief of the Ugandan people; in BG, a title awarded to charismatic black politicians

Kitty/Regent	a public bus route, officially "From Kitty to Georgetown via Regent Street"
laloff	to relax in a laid-back posture
Legco, Leg Co	Legislative Council, for the making and enactment of laws in a British colony
mad bull	a traditional character dancer in a masquerade band
metem, metagee	a dish, the main ingredient being boiled plantain
Mother Sally	a traditional character dancer in a masquerade band
Pakaraimas	Guyana's main mountain range
patwa	a small olive-green fish, very tasty, lives in swamps and canals
plimpla, plimpler	prickly pear, a thorny bush
pork-knocker	an independent prospector for gold or diamonds in the Guyanese Interior, named for the prospectors' regular diet of wild pig
pot salt	ubiquitous, involved in everything
Potaro	a river in the Pakaraimas
psidium	governor-plum
rap-bob-a-pool	a card game sometimes played for 25 cent stakes, the equivalent of a shilling, or bob
Shakira	Guyana's most renowned beauty, a Miss World runner-up who married the British film star, now Sir Michael Caine
shanto	a ballad-like song with a narrative content
simatoo	a popular edible fruit resembling passion-fruit
spit press	gossip network
steups	to make a disapproving sound by sucking the teeth
tawa	an iron plate used by Hindus for baking bread
wallaba	a forest-tree yielding tough, straight-grained timber widely used for posts and fencing
Warrau	an Amerindian people inhabiting the Orinoco Delta and northwest Guyana, noted for boat-building
yawarie	manicou, a kind of opossum